TED TAYLER

A NORMAL NOVEMBER

BOOKS

By Ted Tayler

The Freeman Files

Red Herring Season

Gathering Clouds

Still Standing

Vinci Books

vinci-books.com

Published by Vinci Books Ltd in 2025

1

A CIP catalogue record for this book is available from the British Library.

Paperback ISBN: 9781036705015

Chapter One

Thursday, 30 August 2018

GUS FREEMAN ARRIVED at the Old Police Station office first thing. He had a list of things he needed to deal with after the excitement of last night.

John Ferris had delivered Blessing Umeh to the safety of his Worton farm once he'd persuaded her that Jamie Banks-Trewick and his men had work to do. His wife, Jackie, was waiting patiently in the kitchen to shower Blessing with a lengthy cuddle, a hot drink, and the offer of food despite the lateness of the hour.

"We were so worried," said Jackie. "Thank goodness you're safe."

"I was stupid," said Blessing. "I thought I could prove how someone had done what seemed impossible. How would I know the killer would drive past the main road and spot my Micra on the skyline? Perhaps, I was unlucky, but I should never have gone onto the Plain alone."

"Where are Gus and Suzie?" asked Jackie.

1

"They should get here in a few minutes," said John. "Gus is bringing Blessing's car back. Although, you won't need it for a day or two, young lady. Do what your boss said and rest up before returning to work on Monday."

Blessing sighed.

"I'll miss out on the fun," said Blessing. "A good night's sleep, and I'll be raring to go."

"You've had a shock, Blessing," said Jackie. "That's bound to catch up with you when the adrenaline rush fades. Gus is right. Take your time, enjoy a long weekend, and you'll be firing on four cylinders again."

"That sounds like Suzie's VW racing up the drive," said John. "Will she never learn?"

Jackie coughed a warning. Gus and Suzie had told them about the baby, but there was over a week before Suzie's twelve-week scan and any official announcement. John sat down and waited for Gus and Suzie to come indoors. He knew his place.

Jackie didn't let her daughter and partner escape her kitchen without questions and refreshments. Gus had groaned as he realised it was two o'clock when he and Suzie reached the bungalow in Urchfont.

Suzie seemed content to write it off as good training for next year.

Gus hadn't been surprised to be the first to arrive in the office today. Sleep hadn't come easily last night. He knew they could so easily have lost a valued team member. One by one, the rest of his Crime Review Team rode in the lift to the first floor.

"No sign of Blessing yet, guv?" asked Neil Davis, who was last to put in an appearance for a change.

"Now everyone's here, Neil. I'll explain what happened to her last night," said Gus.

Neil, Luke, Lydia, and Alex sat quietly and listened as Gus told the tale.

"Blessing's okay; that's the key thing," said Lydia.

"We no longer have a case to solve," said Neil. "I didn't expect to hear that this morning."

"No," said Luke. "Every lead we followed went nowhere. So I wonder what prompted Blessing to go it alone?"

"It's not something I recommend," said Gus. "Blessing knows now it was an unnecessary risk. She won't do it again. There's no point getting our files updated before Blessing can offer her invaluable contribution," he said. "We deserve a break. Please make the most of it. Who knows what our next case will bring? I suggest you clear the decks to prepare for next week and then get off home. I don't want to see any of you until Monday morning. I need to make a couple of phone calls, and then I'll follow you."

It did not surprise Gus that there were no objections to a brief holiday. Everyone was as shocked as he was at the sudden turn of events and naturally concerned about their absent colleague. As he searched for the contact details for Corinne Wallington, his phone rang. Geoff Mercer had heard from the security people at Bournemouth Airport.

Oscar Wallington was queuing to board an EasyJet flight to Belfast International when a vigilant officer spotted the fugitive and arrested him. Security personnel later searched his Land Rover Defender in the Long Stay car park and found a twelve-inch long iron bar hidden in a compartment under the driver's seat.

"Many thanks, Geoff," said Gus. "I'll pass the good news onto the team."

"The killer didn't make his escape then, guv?" asked Luke.

"No," said Gus. "If he'd reached the countryside near Portadown, his chances of evading capture would have improved markedly. Wallington knew the area well after serving there as a soldier and spending holidays with the family at the property owned by Corinne's parents. That brings me to my next task. I must put his long-suffering wife in the picture."

Gus called Corinne and relayed the details of Oscar's capture, but he didn't mention the discovery of the murder weapon. Life had changed dramatically for Oscar's wife and two sons in the past twenty-four hours. He didn't need to rub their noses in it.

"Thank you for calling, Mr Freeman," said Corinne. "No doubt, the police would have officially sent someone to inform me in time."

"I thought you deserved to hear it from me. What will you do now?" asked Gus.

"We'll get out from under Patrick's feet," said Corinne. "I'll take his younger brother, Charles, back to the Lodge now the danger has passed. Oscar's employers need to know what's happened. That's not a conversation I expected to have. I enjoyed our time there and hoped we'd stay for many years."

Gus tried to think of something positive that might come of the sorry affair but failed. The manor house needed a new farm manager, and the accommodation at the Lodge went with the job. Her husband was in custody, about to be charged with the murder of Kendal Guthrie. With other possible charges to follow.

Corinne Wallington thanked him again and ended the call. Gus imagined her first call would be to her parents. She and Charles would need a roof over their heads before too long. At least some of the family would make it to Ireland.

Neil was the first to leave the office.

"I changed the filters in the Gaggia, guv," he said. "Alex and Lydia wanted to work on the maps we had on the walls. More than my life's worth to get between those two."

"We'll see you on Monday, Neil," said Gus. "Give our best wishes to Melody."

"Fingers crossed the temperature drops, and she can get a good night's sleep, guv,"

Neil was soon in the lift and heading for the car park. Gus looked around the room. The others wouldn't be far behind him.

"Shall I hang onto these maps, guv?" asked Lydia. "Divya went to a lot of trouble producing them. They might come in handy if we have another murder from the Plain to solve."

"Remove the items we added," said Gus. "Clean one up as best you can and store it in the stationery cabinet with the rest we've gathered over the months. The rest can go into the recycling bins in the corner of the car park downstairs. It won't hurt our image if the locals see we're doing our bit."

Alex and Lydia left together ten minutes later. Luke Sherman wandered across to join Gus.

"Something on your mind, Luke?" asked Gus.

"I had a phone call last night from a former colleague. He transferred to West Mercia Police eighteen months ago. We attended the same weapons training course. They've got a vacancy for a training officer, and he wondered if I was interested."

"Salary-wise, it wouldn't attract you, surely?" asked Gus.

"No, but the hours would be more predictable, which

solves Nicky's problems," said Luke. "He wouldn't have any trouble finding employment if we re-located, and there's more nightlife in the Midlands."

"Have you spoken to anyone at London Road?"

Luke shook his head.

"I'll use the extra free time this weekend to think things through," said Luke. "If I decide to put my name forward, I'll tell DS Mercer."

"I don't want to see you leave," said Gus. "You're three years younger than Suzie Ferris. With the breadth of experience you've gained since becoming a sergeant, I'm sure Geoff Mercer has a career path in mind. But don't make a hasty decision. We've all suffered relationship issues because of the unsocial hours we work, but something usually turns up that offers a solution."

"Let's be honest, guv," said Luke. "If a DI role popped up from London Road, Alex would be first in line. Either that or they would bring someone in from another region, as they did with Grace Packenham. I'll see you on Monday."

As the lift doors closed behind Luke, Gus sat in the office alone and wondered what had possessed him to return to work. He'd left this angst behind him four years ago. Gus thought back to his first evening in the Bear Hotel with Geoff Mercer when the Detective Superintendent outlined his hopes and dreams for the Crime Review Team and urged Gus to come and work for him.

Gus had decided to give it a whirl. Retirement wasn't all it was cracked up to be, especially after Tess had died. So when he'd met with Alex, Neil, and Lydia, he imagined the first to fly the nest would be the fiery red-haired female.

Because of her qualifications and background, Kenneth Truelove had already warned him that the university graduate was on a fast-track programme. The modern police service pushed for a more diverse image, and Lydia had plenty to offer on that score.

Perhaps it was inevitable following the team's early run of successful investigations that the pressures would grow. Both internal and external pressure, as teams around the county and beyond spotted talent they could use. Any team member might want to spread their wings, and who was he to stand in their way if that was their decision?

A second phone call interrupted his gloomy vision of the future.

Geoff Mercer had another update.

Engineers working under Jamie Banks-Trewick had recovered human remains from a gully near the boundary of land belonging to the farm on Durrington Down. Subject to official confirmation, the Military Police believed the remains were those of Private John Winslow. He died from blunt force trauma to the skull.

Gus listened to Geoff Mercer's upbeat report in silence.

"Everything okay, Gus?" he asked. "I thought the second piece of good news in one day would be a matter to celebrate."

"What do you make of Luke Sherman?" asked Gus.

"An excellent young officer with a bright future," said Geoff. "Why do you ask?"

"Are you planning to move him to a more senior role soon?"

"I don't know what you've heard, Gus, but no, Kenneth and I are delighted with where Luke is at present. We're in no rush to change a winning team."

"Luke's partner would prefer they spent more time together. Nicky works nine to five. You know how it goes."

"We've been there, Gus. Christine had the same reaction to the long hours and sullen moods when I was younger. It's something Luke, Neil, and the others have to go through at certain stages in their careers."

"Luke heard of a vacancy in West Mercia," said Gus. "It would be a step sideways at best, and at worst, it could harm his progress for good. So I'd prefer him to stay with us for the foreseeable future."

"Look, you know Kenneth's role as Chief Constable is a stop-gap measure to calm the storm after the rapid turnover Wiltshire Police experienced in that role. Who knows what will happen when he retires? In eighteen months or two years, what will you feel like? Maybe you will be ready to hand in that consultant's ID card and return to your allotment full-time. If the new boss wants to keep the Crime Review Team, it will need a DI at the helm. That's a carrot to dangle in front of Luke Sherman."

"Luke thinks Alex Hardy will be more likely to get a promotion before him, Geoff," said Gus. "Or you might bring someone in from outside, as you did with Ms Packenham."

"You needn't fret about Grace getting the lead job with CRT, Gus," laughed Geoff. "She's good, but not that good. Alex always expressed a wish to return to his old job as a motorcycle pursuit rider. That may be too big an ask, but Alex is a good number two. He's more of a plodder, like Neil Davis. I won't write the two of them off as having got as far as they're going to get, but Luke and Lydia are much better prospects."

"Despite having done something reckless last night," said Gus, "DC Umeh is one to watch. I reckon Blessing has star quality at twenty-two for what it's worth."

"If you rate her highly, Gus, then Kenneth and I will listen. Keep me in the picture with Luke Sherman. We need to help him decide to stay with you for at least eighteen months. I guess the next time I'll see you will be Monday lunchtime?"

"That's the plan, Geoff," said Gus.

"Have an enjoyable weekend then, and well done again this week. Another rotten apple removed, and another case that won't haunt the original detectives until they reach the Pearly Gates."

Gus decided there was nothing to keep him in the office today. As for what he might say in eighteen months, that was a different matter. Gus took one last look around and headed for the lift. He had the entire afternoon to himself. The weather was fine, and the allotment was as good a place to spend it as any.

Friday, 31 August – Sunday, 2 September

BLESSING UMEH HAD SPENT two lazy days on the farm at Worton. Jackie had been right about delayed shock. Blessing stayed in bed most of Thursday morning, and when she wasn't sleeping, she sat in the kitchen with her landlady, drinking coffee and watching Jackie baking.

Jackie had asked Blessing if she was going to call her parents.

"They won't have heard what happened on the Plain," said Blessing. "My father would drive here and insist I quit my job at once. So no, it has to be our secret."

When Blessing received a text on her mobile phone late on Thursday afternoon, she had hoped it was Gus relenting, saying she could return to work on Friday. The text wasn't from Gus.

Jackie heard the delighted squeal and turned to see Blessing punching the air.

"That was good news, I take it?" she said with a smile.

"Jamie wants to know if it's okay to visit me tomorrow afternoon," said Blessing. "Do you mind?"

"Not at all," said Jackie. "I can't wait to meet him. John told me he was a charming young man, and even Suzie had to admit he was handsome."

"Jamie's just what I was looking for," said Blessing. "My knight in shining armour."

"What about the young man your family wanted you to meet on Sunday?" asked Jackie.

"Ekene Kanu? He needs a woman who will look after him day and night, bear him children, and never speak out of turn. It wouldn't work between us; we're from different worlds."

Jackie smiled to herself as she kneaded her pastry dough. John didn't know it yet, but they were going to make themselves scarce on Friday afternoon. Blessing and her dreamboat needed to be alone.

When Blessing wandered into the kitchen on Friday morning, Jackie was taking a well-earned break.

"I don't need to ask if you slept better last night," she said. "I was just going to make myself a coffee."

"Is that eleven o'clock?" asked Blessing. "Half the day's gone."

"What time did Jamie say he would get here?"

"Between two and three," said Blessing. "He's working this morning and hoping to get away early for a change."

"Do you want any breakfast?" asked Jackie.

"I'm starving," admitted Blessing, "But I'll wait until lunchtime now. Coffee would be perfect for the time being, thanks."

"John's driving me to Amesbury this afternoon," Jackie said. "We'll not get back until late. Do you think you can cook something for the two of you? Or will you venture into Devizes for a meal?"

"I don't know how long Jamie can stay," said Blessing. "He's on call in case there's another incident like the one he responded to on Wednesday evening."

"John will be in for his midday meal in an hour," said Jackie. "Have you got your appetite back, Blessing?"

"You bet," said Blessing.

"Why not spend the afternoon in the orchard?" said Jackie. "It's cooler, and you know there's plenty of food in this kitchen to snack on if the two of you get hungry."

John and Jackie left in the Land Rover before one o'clock. Blessing showered and tried on half a dozen dresses before deciding which one to wear. At two o'clock, she stood by the kitchen door, trying to hear the sound of an approaching car. She didn't have long to wait.

Blessing's heart flipped when Jamie got out of the car and walked towards her. The tight-fitting white t-shirt, black jeans, and aviator shades were a look to grace the catwalk in Paris or Milan. Jamie removed his sunglasses and smiled.

"It appears you've fully recovered from the other night," he said. "You look stunning."

"So do you," said Blessing. "I wondered what you looked like out of uniform."

Jamie laughed.

"So, this is where you live? Do I get the grand tour?"

"You've spent ages on Salisbury Plain," said Blessing. "Once you've seen one farm, you've seen them all. So why don't we visit the orchard at the back of the farmhouse? It's shaded, quiet, and the perfect spot on a warm afternoon. I often sit there to read or to chat with Jackie, my landlady. Can I get you a drink?"

"A cold beer would be great," said Jamie as he followed Blessing along the path at the side of the farmhouse.

Blessing turned around to look at him.

"Well, I didn't plan to drive back to Bulford for ages," Jamie said.

"That's a relief," said Blessing. "In that case, I'll have a glass of wine too."

Time flies when you're having fun, and it was early evening when Blessing snapped a selfie of her and Jamie lying on a rug under the branches of an apple tree.

"Facebook?" asked Jamie.

"No," said Blessing. "I thought I should send it to someone my parents know."

Blessing sent the photo with no words. The message was simple. Ekene Kanu was now aware he was surplus to requirements. Jamie BT was a great kisser, and Blessing Umeh was not looking for a make-do husband.

When John and Jackie Ferris returned to Worton Farm later that evening, the farmyard was empty.

"I'd better wander around to check everything's secure," said John. "See you in ten minutes."

Jackie went indoors and found Blessing sitting in the kitchen.

"How did it go?" asked Jackie.

"It couldn't have been better," said Blessing. "I hope my parents forgive me."

"The heart wants what the heart wants," said Jackie, hugging Blessing.

"Did you and John get what you wanted in Amesbury?" asked Blessing.

"We drove around for a while, drank in a pub, and then

sat on a park bench like we did when we were sixteen. We just wanted to give you two time alone."

ON SUNDAY MORNING, Blessing drove to Englishcombe village, her parents' house. She attended morning service at St Peter's Church with Kelechi and Maryam, then returned home for lunch.

"I thought you told me Ekene Kanu was going to be there this morning," said Blessing as her father carved the roast beef.

"Ekene called yesterday," said her father. "He said he was indisposed. I said I hoped he got well soon. I got the distinct impression his indisposition could be permanent. Do you know anything about that?"

"I never met the man in person," said Blessing. "How could I know what made him change his mind?"

"We didn't have time to speak much on Wednesday evening," said Maryam. "I hope Mr Freeman's not working you too hard?"

Blessing squeezed her mother's hand. Maryam hadn't told Kelechi that she'd asked her mother for Ekene's phone number.

"Mr Freeman is looking after me, don't worry. I have much to be grateful for, and my trip on Wednesday evening bore fruit. I hope my work-life balance will improve in the months ahead."

Monday, 3 September 2018

"WHAT'S on the agenda for today, Gus?" asked Suzie as she popped two slices of bread into the toaster.

"We didn't hear any negative reports from John and Jackie over the weekend," said Gus, "so I expect to see Blessing fighting fit and back in the office. She needs to update our digital files on the Guthrie case as soon as possible. Then, it won't take the rest of us long to fill in the blanks. I fully expect to take the completed files to London Road before noon. The office is as tidy as it's been in weeks, so while I collect our next case file from Kenneth, the others will probably relax and pepper Blessing with questions about her few hours of excitement."

"We used to call that skiving in the old days," said Suzie. "I can't recall the last time we had free time at London Road."

"That's the Packenham effect, I presume?"

"Grace's relentless," said Suzie. "She wants to turn the place into a lean, mean crime-fighting machine."

"Ms Packenham reports to Geoff Mercer," said Gus. "A man who has carried more than a few extra pounds for the past two decades. I never thought Geoff would be the sort to follow the 'don't do as I do, do as I tell you' principle. The lady is a loose cannon. Someone needs to have a quiet word in Geoff's ear."

"I wonder who you have in mind?" laughed Suzie.

"Has Geoff found anything new to add to your workload?" asked Gus.

"On Friday afternoon, he mentioned the PCC had raised the subject of thefts from vehicles," said Suzie. "Statistics showed an increase from nine to ten per day across the county compared to last year. Most of these incidents occur in beauty spots and are from insecure vehicles or those that have valuables on display. He asked me to run a crime prevention campaign urging motorists to lock their vehicles and keep belongings out of sight."

"It will keep you out of mischief," said Gus.

"Even if it's Common Sense, Room 101," said Suzie. "Are you going to eat that second slice of toast?"

"Not today," said Gus. "I may bump into Ms Packenham later. I don't want to give her any ideas."

They left the bungalow at eight-fifteen on the dot and drove in convoy towards Devizes.

When Suzie turned into the London Road car park, Gus gave her a wave and carried on towards the Old Police Station office seven miles away.

He had achieved a lot since Thursday lunchtime. The allotment was now on par with Bert Penman's plot for the first time in months. All the jobs he'd put off for weeks had been finished. Tess's climbing roses on the side of the bungalow could now enjoy a controlled flourish with a newly added wire framework. The wooden bench on the edge of the front lawn had gained a fresh coat of wood stain.

Gus had stood in the doorway of the second bedroom on Friday afternoon, wondering whether to make a start on re-decorating it, ready for the new arrival. But instead, he decided against making unilateral decisions until Suzie reached home.

Suzie had accompanied him to the allotment, as the weekend weather had been conducive to spending time outdoors. Gus persuaded her to sit and watch him work. Suzie agreed, as long as Gus let her drive into Devizes on Saturday afternoon to pick up an armful of brochures from various DIY stores.

"If I'm to sit and watch you work for several hours today and tomorrow, I can plan for the first weekend when the weather forces us indoors," she said. "Do I have a budget?"

Gus had stopped weeding and thought for a second.

"I've ignored every budget London Road has ever set. I told Geoff Mercer when I returned to work that if they wanted the job done right, it would cost what it would cost, and I don't see any reason to work to different limits at home."

"That's the right answer," said Suzie, dropping the cheaper brochures onto the grass beside her chair.

Although Gus knew he had earned brownie points with Suzie with his reply, he spent much of Saturday afternoon thinking of Luke Sherman and Geoff Mercer's comments when he'd spoken to him on Thursday morning.

Somehow, he had to persuade Luke to stay.

Geoff thought Luke was a potential Detective Inspector and the prime candidate to succeed Gus as head of the Crime Review Team when the time came. Gus couldn't fault the logic. After all, Kenneth Truelove was under orders from his wife to retire as soon as possible. The thrill of being the wife of a Chief Constable would only last so long. Geoff's view was it had a lifespan of eighteen months, two years at the most.

The storm clouds would gather, and Gus's protection would become vulnerable once Kenneth's protection disappeared. However, DI Sherman could confidently take things forward if the team had proved it deserved to stay in existence through a string of solid successes.

Geoff's other comments had given things Gus hadn't considered an uncomfortable clarity. Gus had never been a fan of the annual appraisals introduced at Bourne Hill during the latter part of his time there. Gus believed a team was like a car with four wheels. None of those wheels was worth any more than the other.

Now he had learned that the top brass at London Road viewed people like Alex Hardy and Neil Davis as less valuable than Luke Sherman. That gave him a problem he didn't need. How could he tinker with the team dynamic, so Luke felt the love while keeping Alex and Neil happy too? They weren't daft. He'd always treated everyone alike since they started working together. Those two would soon wonder what was behind any changes, no matter how subtle.

As he slowed at the traffic lights near the village of Seend, Gus thought about Lydia and Blessing. Geoff Mercer intimated he was more likely to find openings for those two. They had tremendous potential. Ten minutes later, Gus parked the Focus in the empty bay behind the Old Police Station and steeled himself for what lay ahead. As a young lad, he'd never mastered the art of juggling, and at sixty-two, he was unlikely to be able to add it to his skill set.

Gus found the rest of the team gathered around Blessing Umeh's desk. He heard his young Detective Constable mention Jamie Banks-Trewick twice and wondered whether the Second Lieutenant from the Military Police Special Investigations Branch had visited Blessing since the early hours of Thursday. It had been hard enough prising them apart and persuading her to get into John Ferris's Land Rover.

"Morning, guv," said Lydia. "All present and correct. Blessing solved the murder and found a boyfriend. All on the same night."

"It's good to see you looking refreshed and ready for a

new challenge," said Gus. "Have you started updating those files yet?"

"We only arrived a minute ahead of you, guv," said Neil. "We've hardly had time to do much more than hear about Blessing's weekend."

"How were your parents, Blessing?" asked Gus.

"What they don't know about the details of Wednesday night won't hurt them, guv. I was a dutiful daughter and attended church in Englishcombe, and then I spent the afternoon with them before returning to Worton Farm. I should finish my updates by eleven o'clock if that fits your timetable."

"That will be perfect, Blessing," said Gus. "How about the rest of you? Any problems with meeting that deadline?"

Nobody protested, so Gus got stuck into completing a report on his contributions to the case from Wednesday afternoon onwards. One hour later, Alex and Lydia offered to get coffee for the team. Blessing was still recounting her adventures in the middle of Salisbury Plain while Neil and Luke read through the Guthrie case notes for the third time.

"Has anyone notified the detectives from the original investigation?" asked Neil.

"Keith Porter is still at Bourne Hill," said Luke. "Gus and Blessing visited Maxine Coleman last week at home with her baby."

"That's right. Maxine's a Devereux now, married to that rugby player. Gus might think she'll want to learn we've wrapped up the case. I'll ask him before he shoots off to Devizes."

"I'd like to know what Helen Guthrie made of it," said Luke. "The files show Gus heard from Geoff Mercer after we left here on Thursday. The SIB people found human remains on one farm Kendall Guthrie submitted a bid for before he died. Wallington had killed before. He must have suspected Guthrie would discover his secret. I was reading an article at the weekend, and if Helen Guthrie had plans to carry on what her father started and sell that land to developers, she'd have to think again. The MoD built dozens of temporary buildings near the garrison camps during WWII. Then, after the war, they bulldozed the site and buried everything underground. The farmers who lived and worked there struggled to grow anything, so they used it for grazing sheep and cows. The article I read reckoned asbestos and lead have tainted the land. No way could anyone build on it."

"You know what that means," said Neil. "Wallington didn't need to panic when he heard Guthrie mention the farm was among the batch he'd applied to buy. The odds of anyone testing soil samples and then uncovering those remains were tiny. Gus's report said they found the remains in a gully on the edge of the property. Private Winslow was reported as AWOL twenty years ago, and nobody had ever thought to look for a body."

"So, Kendal Guthrie didn't need to die," said Luke.

"If Oscar Wallington hadn't done it, someone else would have," said Neil with a shrug. "He was universally disliked. That's not something I would want on my headstone."

"My report is ready to go, guv," said Blessing.

"With ten minutes to spare," said Neil. "Luke and I wondered whether you wanted us to inform DI Porter and Mrs Devereux, guv?"

"I don't think Keith Porter will bother Neil," said Gus, "but call him, by all means. Call Maxine too, for definite. It might convince her to return to work after her maternity leave. We live in hope."

"How do you think Ms Guthrie will react to the news that the farmland opposite Glenhead Farm is riddled with asbestos and lead?" asked Luke.

"Which renders it unsuitable for development," added Neil.

"I think you can leave that one to me," said Gus. "I owe her one."

Chapter Two

GUS SKIPPED into the lift with the Guthrie file folder and whistled a cheerful tune as he emerged into the car park. He stood by the open driver's door of the Focus, waiting in vain for the temperature inside to drop to bearable. Time was pressing, so he reversed out of his parking bay and headed for the exit.

It was fifteen minutes to twelve when he turned off the London Road into the Wiltshire Police HQ visitor's car park. He sat and thought about Maxine Devereux. What if she decided to be a stay-at-home Mum? Nothing wrong with that, of course, if that was her choice. Even if she was depriving the county of the services of a first-class detective.

If Maxine decided she would enjoy a return to work eighteen months or two years from now, where might she be a good fit as a Detective Inspector? Perhaps he should start dropping hints to Geoff Mercer that Maxine would make a better replacement for him and the CRT when he finally got put out to grass.

Did that mean he was coming around to the idea Luke

could transfer to West Mercia? These personnel problems were a nuisance. His sole focus needed to be on whatever case the Chief Constable handed him in the next half-hour. Gus would never admit to Suzie that multi-tasking was easier for her than for him, but he found it impossible in this arena.

Gus trotted up the steps to the main door and spotted an older face on the Reception desk. This morning, access to the first floor without pranks or mishaps should be a breeze. Within seconds, he signed in and took the stairs two at a time.

"It's a warm one this morning, Mr Freeman," said Kassie Trotter. "Did you hear? August was the warmest month on record in England."

"Too warm for baking, I presume?" asked Gus.

"I'm into skinny-baking these days, Mr Freeman," said Kassie. "I told you last week."

Gus had tried to rid himself of the image Kassie had planted but failed.

"The end product tasted better than ever, Kassie," he said. "I left work early to allow myself time to enjoy the experience. You're a genius."

"Do you want to know what I have for you in my drawers, Mr Freeman?"

"That's not what Kassie meant, Gus," said Vera Butler, who suddenly appeared on his left-hand side. "Kassie concentrated on a lighter bite in deference to the warm weather. I'm sure you'll enjoy a slice of her summer berry cake."

"I'll keep an eye out for the office mafia and collect my treat after meeting with Kenneth," said Gus. "How are things in your world, Vera?"

"Monty's having issues with several of his tenants," said

Vera. "I'm glad I'm out of it. You remember what he was like; a prince one year and a pauper the next. He's panicking over what the eventual Brexit deal will hold."

"I'm guessing several properties he bought to let got snapped up by people from Poland and the Baltic states," said Gus. "If the divorce is painful, there's a risk they'll return home, and he'll lose a significant proportion of his income."

"Exactly," said Vera. "Some younger women have jumped ship already without clearing their rent arrears."

"I'm surprised Monty stood for any arrears based on what you've told me."

"He's a single man these days, Gus," said Vera. "I suspect he had an ulterior motive."

"Has he contacted you?" asked Gus.

"Monty knows better than to try anything like that with me, Gus," said Vera. "No, he's sneaky. He dropped by my parent's home to give them a sob story about how hard life was for a hard-working businessman in the UK."

"Monty didn't ask for financial help, but he sowed the seeds," said Gus.

"That's typical of Monty," said Vera. "It's always someone else's fault when a get-rich scheme turns turtle. My father sensed Monty felt this latest downturn in his fortunes wouldn't have happened if we were still married."

"No doubt Monty got short shrift from your father?"

"My father bailed Monty out frequently, as you know. He won't receive any more help from that quarter. I feel sorry for Monty, but he brings it on himself."

"You were married to the guy for half the time you've been on this earth, Vera. So it's only natural you still take an interest in what's happening with him. He's the father of your children. What's done is done. You have your life to lead now, and Monty has to fight his own battles."

"You'd better get over to Kenneth's office," said Vera. "You'll be late. Thanks for taking the trouble to listen."

"What are friends for, Vera?" said Gus. He spotted Kassie Trotter pointing to the second and third drawers on a filing cabinet by her desk and gave her a reassuring wave.

Geoff Mercer emerged from Kenneth's old office and caught Gus before reaching the Chief Constable's door.

"Any progress?" he asked.

"With Luke Sherman, d'you mean?" asked Gus. "I haven't spoken with him this morning."

"Don't leave it too long, Gus," said Geoff. "West Mercia was keen to secure a deal when they put the feelers out to me a while back. So if they hear a whisper Luke's unsettled in his CRT role and interested in a move to the Midlands, they'll snap him up before you can say West Bromwich Albion."

"We've got ages then, Geoff," said Gus.

The Chief Constable was at his desk when they walked through the door.

Gus handed the Kendal Guthrie file to Kenneth Truelove.

"Another one bites the dust, sir,"

"Mercer tells me this success could have come at a high price, Freeman. It would help if you kept better control over your people. That's not your only fault. At the outset, I said you needed to take a serving officer with you whenever you interviewed a witness or a suspect. I received a complaint from Helen Guthrie at the weekend. She thought your manner surly and confrontational."

"It takes two to tango, sir," said Gus. "She started it, wheeling in her farm manager and solicitor for what was supposed to be an informal chat. They weren't interested in offering any help to find her father's killer."

"I hope you won't make a habit of flying solo, Freeman," said the Chief Constable. "It sends the wrong message to the junior members of your team, evidenced by the calamity that almost befell DC Umeh."

"I'll be more cautious in the future, sir," said Gus, deciding not to mention he'd also visited Dave Vickers and Oscar Wallington alone the same day.

"How is DC Umeh now?" asked Kenneth.

"Fighting fit, sir," said Gus. "Blessing had Thursday and Friday off work. I believe she drove to visit her parents yesterday and seemed fine this morning."

"You should remind DC Umeh that her well-being is important to us, Freeman. If she needs to speak to someone about the emotional arousal from the events of Wednesday evening, then you must make sure that happens. Blessing may look fine on the surface, but frights such as that can lead to PTSD."

"Got it, sir," said Gus. "I understand she's spoken to someone already. From snatches of conversation I caught in the office this morning, good progress has been made, and someone has a firm grip on her emotions."

"Right then, perhaps we can park that matter for now. I want you both to watch this CCTV clip. That's if I can remember how to work this blessed remote control. The quality of the image isn't great, but you will get the gist of what's occurring."

Gus and Geoff watched the screen, and Kenneth provided a running commentary.

"We have a couple of likely lads, bold as brass, stealing a catalytic converter in broad daylight. This white van pulls up behind the target vehicle; its driver and passenger get out. The passenger walks by to look at the car and check for nosy passers-by. Then the driver fetches a jack from the back of the van. He sets to work at the side of the car. The passenger removes a saw from his hooded jacket, and off he goes. You don't need to put a clock on it. Thirty-one seconds for a piece of kit that could fetch at least one thousand pounds depending on the damage caused as they remove it."

"Inside two minutes, they were in the van and driving away," said Geoff Mercer.

"Although the image was poor, even I could read the number plate of the van," said Gus.

"False plates," said Kenneth, "belonging to a VW Passat reported stolen seven weeks before the theft. Both men wore hooded jackets, which proved impossible to identify."

"Both men were white," said Geoff. "The driver was perhaps six feet tall, while his colleague was six to eight inches shorter. Despite the baggy clothing, we can make assumptions about their build, but there's nothing for the Hub to use to match them with anyone in our databases."

"When and where did this theft occur?" asked Gus.

"Towards the end of October, two years ago," said Kenneth.

"There must be more to this than the theft of a few car parts," said Gus.

"They may not look much," scoffed the Chief Constable, "but it's big business. Those catalytic converters contain two valuable metals, rhodium and palladium, and the price of those metals is on the increase. That's attracted the interest of organised crime gangs who have acquired specialist tools to remove converters from cars. We've visited the local scrap metal dealers, warning them to be mindful when offered converters or exhaust systems. Some will contact us if they suspect they could have been stolen, but other dealers aren't so scrupulous."

"Where did the theft take place?" asked Gus. "Those buildings in the background look familiar. Are we in Swindon?"

"Just off Station Road," said Geoff.

"That is brazen," said Gus. "Right. Can you tell me why I had to watch this CCTV clip?"

"I want you to take a second look at the murder of Richard Chaloner," said Kenneth, handing Gus a copy of the file. "He owned a garage, perhaps half a mile from where this theft occurred. Chaloner was forty-four years old and had recently married a forty-one-year-old divorcee, Eve Allsopp. Chaloner had been a single man until the wedding, which took place six months before he died. The victim was last seen alive at ten to six on Monday, the seventh of November 2016. Chaloner ran a small business that handled car body repairs, MOTs, that sort of thing. He had two employees. Matt Merchant, twenty-nine, and Harry Simpkins, sixty-one. Both men had worked for Chaloner for over ten years. Simpkins left work at the usual time at half-past five and walked to his home in Alfred Street."

"I wonder why Merchant stayed late?" asked Gus.

"I'll come to that in a moment, Freeman. Chaloner cycled to and from work," said the Chief Constable. "Richard and Eve Chaloner had moved into a house on Shrivenham Road, the other side of the County Ground from the railway station."

"The County Ground is where Swindon Town play, Gus," said Geoff.

"I'm not a fan," said Gus, "but I know where they play, Geoff. Gary Mallinder and Ian Hewson went to watch a match there. The stadium is only ten minutes from Gentle

Touch, the massage parlour where Laura Mallinder worked. I'm familiar with the district."

Kenneth Truelove continued with his introduction to the new case.

"As Merchant was leaving, he spotted Chaloner's bicycle had a puncture. He returned to the office, where his boss checked invoices and completed worksheets. Chaloner went outside with Merchant to inspect the damage. It wasn't a puncture; someone had deliberately slashed the tyre. Matt Merchant offered his boss a lift home, but Chaloner told him he'd finish the paperwork, fix the problem himself, and he'd see him in the morning."

"Did Merchant see anyone near the garage when he left?" asked Gus.

"At ten to six on a miserable, wet Monday evening in November," said Kenneth. "What do you think?"

"Too early for dog walkers," said Gus. "Anyone with any sense would have been tucked up indoors eating a warm meal."

"Matt Merchant was first to arrive at eight o'clock the following day," said Kenneth. "it did not surprise him to see the boss's bicycle in its usual spot. He didn't give it a second glance, parked his car, and entered the garage by the side door."

"Did he have a key?" asked Gus.

"Both Merchant and Simpkins had keys for the side door and the office," said Kenneth. "Whoever arrived first went inside and got things ready for the working day. Chaloner was a good boss, according to his employees. His customers appreciated the warm, friendly atmosphere he encouraged, and repeat business kept the little enterprise busy. The side door was open, and Merchant looked towards the office, expecting to find Chaloner sitting at his desk. The office was empty, but the lights were on. Merchant heard a sound outside. It was Harry Simpkins arriving for work. Simpkins flicked the light switches to illuminate the main part of the building as soon as he stepped inside to join Merchant. They saw Richard Chaloner's body lying between two cars they had worked on the previous afternoon. Simpkins walked towards the body, but Merchant told him to stay clear. He went outside and used his mobile to phone the police."

"It makes a change for a member of the public to preserve the integrity of a crime scene," said Gus. "Merchant sounds like an upright citizen, am I right?"

"He had a few brushes with the law as a juvenile," said Kenneth, "but marriage and three kids have had a positive effect."

"He hasn't had time to go off the rails," said Gus. "Hold it a moment. I'm forgetting someone. You said Chaloner married six months before he died. So why didn't his wife raise the alarm when he didn't arrive home?"

"Eve was in Halkidiki with three friends from work on a seven-day hen night," said Kenneth. "They're all the rage these days. I was lucky to get a three-hour stag do."

"Me too," said Gus and Geoff in unison.

"That must have burst the party balloons when news filtered through," said Gus. "Who caught this case from Gablecross?"

"The SIO was DI Raj Sengupta," said the Chief Constable.

"Ah yes, the cybercrime team leader," said Gus. "He worked with Jack Sanders. Our paths have crossed."

"I wouldn't want this to escape these four walls," said Kenneth, "but Sengupta is in a better place these days. He performs a valuable role with the cybercrime team but was hopeless out in the field."

"Colonel Sanders was an old-school copper," said Gus. "I can't see him and Raj seeing eye-to-eye. Who else did Raj have on his team?"

"DS Tom Spencer," said Geoff Mercer. "He's from the same mould as Jake Latimer. Rough around the edges, plenty of local knowledge, and not afraid of hard work."

"When you read the murder file, Freeman, you'll see that DS Spencer did most of the leg work. Stuart Fitzwalter was the police surgeon who attended the murder scene at the garage. He determined Chaloner died from a single gunshot to the chest. His killer was no further than three feet away. The time of death was between six and seven in the evening. The killer must have turned off the main lights as they left the garage but left the office lights on."

"Any evidence left at the scene? What was the motive?" asked Gus.

"Forensics found no fingerprints," said Kenneth Truelove. "One possible chance would have been the light switches, but Harry Simpkins obliterated any hope of that. DS Spencer always believed the killer wore gloves, so maybe Simpkins was off the hook. As for motive, Chaloner's wallet was stolen, which his wife believed would have contained less than one hundred pounds. A gold chain her husband always wore around his neck was missing. The killer took a bank card for the garage's business account from the victim's desk and used it to withdraw four hundred pounds from an ATM in the town centre later that evening. Merchant stopped the card on Tuesday morning. The killer never attempted to use it again."

"What happened? Did the victim reveal the PIN without a fight?" asked Gus.

"There were no signs of a struggle," said Kenneth. "Remember, when Merchant left on Monday evening, Chaloner worked in the office. So the card was likely lying on the desk when the killer walked in. Matt Merchant confirmed Chaloner had the PIN written on a scrap of paper pinned to the notice board," said Kenneth.

"Terrific," said Gus. "Chaloner was a very trusting boss. With lax security, both employees could have helped themselves whenever they pleased."

"Come on, Gus," said Geoff. "Merchant said it was a happy work environment. Someone withdrew the money on Monday evening. If Chaloner hadn't died, he would have spotted the missing money once he checked his business account. Small firms such as that live hand-to-mouth these days. I doubt the working balance would have hidden a four hundred-pound black hole."

"How did DI Sengupta approach the case?" asked Gus.

"He treated it as a robbery in the first instance. It seemed logical," said Kenneth.

"An armed robbery in a busy part of Swindon isn't an everyday occurrence," said Gus. "Why did the killer slash the bicycle tyre?"

"The police believed that was a tactic to keep Chaloner from leaving with his employees," said Kenneth. "The killer waited until Merchant left the premises. He wanted to guarantee Chaloner was alone."

"What was Sengupta's first move?" asked Gus.

"Sengupta organised his uniformed officers on a house-to-house, searching for eyewitnesses. Not to the murder, but someone tampering with Chaloner's bicycle or acting suspiciously in the garage's vicinity."

"Why didn't Chaloner wheel his bike indoors?" asked Gus. "There must have been room, surely?"

"Force of habit," said Kenneth. "Before the wedding, he'd lived in Pinehurst. He had made the two-mile journey every weekday since he opened the business. His bike wasn't one of these top-of-the-range items that demand the rider wear lycra. Instead, it was a bog-standard machine with a comfortable saddle and panniers. Although Chaloner secured it to a metal fence while working inside, he never dreamt anyone would want to steal it. The bike was visible from the pavement, but whoever slashed the tyre had to walk past Merchant's car to reach it."

"Where does Merchant live?" asked Gus.

"Elmina Road, with wife Jess and their three children," said Kenneth.

"Matt Merchant was young and presumably fit," said Gus. "Why drive to work from Elmina Road? It can't be further than a ten-minute walk away. Harry Simpkins walked from Alfred Street, which was as far in the opposite direction."

"Merchant played six-a-side football on Monday evenings," said Kenneth. "He had a fifteen-minute drive out towards Wootton Bassett via Great Western Way. His teammates confirmed he was at the Gerard Buxton Sports Arena between six-thirty and eight-thirty. His alibi was set in concrete, as was Harry Simpkins. Harry's wife, Thelma, said he reached home at twenty minutes to six, as usual, and was eating his dinner at six. They walked the dog together at six-thirty and sat in front of the TV to watch The One Show at seven o'clock. Harry never left the house until ten to eight the following day to walk to work."

"Okay, so what did the interviews with the employees and the house-to-house enquiries throw up?" asked Gus.

"Three persons of interest," said the Chief Constable. "The first man was white, thirty-five to forty-five years old, wearing white overalls. Simpkins told police he turned up at the garage on Monday morning at around eleven o'clock. He hadn't made an appointment and asked Richard Chaloner to look at an intermittent electrical fault on his van. Chaloner pointed out all three of them were busy at present on jobs booked in for regular customers. So they didn't have time to stop. Simpkins was underneath the car he was working on and couldn't see what happened next, but raised voices suggested the guy in white overalls wasn't happy with his boss's reply. When Simpkins next stood up, the van and its driver had left without getting what he wanted. Chaloner was in the office, calling a customer to say his car was ready to collect. He didn't elaborate on the argument with either Merchant or Simpkins."

"Did the police find this painter and decorator, or whatever this tradesperson was?" asked Gus.

"Harry Simpkins was lying on a trolley under the car, Freeman," said Kenneth. "Hardly in a position to identify anyone or spot any writing on the side of the van. Merchant gave a general description of the unexpected visitor to the police. He, too, continued working towards the rear of the garage on a customer's car while the man stayed on the premises. Although he overheard snatches of the conversation, he couldn't give the detectives a name."

"It could be something of nothing," said Geoff Mercer. "Richard Chaloner forgot the episode quickly and got on with his busy workload. It doesn't strike me as being the catalyst for what occurred later that day."

"I'd still want to find out who drove that van," said Gus. "Who else did they put in the frame?"

"The second person was a twenty to twenty-five-year-old white man," said Kenneth. "He was a short, stocky individual with short blonde hair, wearing a navy bomber jacket. This man stood on the opposite side of the road from one o'clock to a few minutes before two."

"Was it Merchant or Simpkins who saw him?" asked Gus.

"It was neither," said Kenneth. "A Mrs Catherine Fryer returned home from her morning shift at a care home in Dean Park and had to step off the pavement to get past him. When she came out again at ten to two to post a letter, the man in the bomber jacket still stood in the same spot. Mrs Fryer returned ten minutes later, and the man had gone."

"Was he another one that got away with no one identifying him?" asked Gus.

"I'm afraid so," said the Chief Constable. "The description was more specific than for the white van man, but Swindon has its fair share of twenty-something white men. The uniformed officers who did the house-to-house were certain he didn't live on the same street as Mrs Fryer, but that was about as much as they could say. Now we come to person of interest number three. He was Afro-Caribbean, twenty-five to thirty, muscular, and wearing dark clothing. Mrs Fryer's neighbour, Stan Jones, seventy-one, saw someone standing on tiptoe to peer through the window on the front door of the garage at four o'clock in the afternoon. Mr Jones was pulling his curtains as the light was fading fast."

"Hang on," said Gus. "I got the impression when the white van man arrived at eleven, he parked and walked off the street straight into the garage to speak to Richard Chaloner. How come the doors were closed?"

"Because of the rain," said Kenneth. "Simpkins and Merchant said that by half-past two, the strength of the wind had increased, and what started as a light shower soon became a downpour. However, the side door was still open if a customer wanted to check work-in-progress or book in a vehicle."

"How long was this chap peering through the window?" asked Gus.

"Only a minute or two," said Kenneth. "Stan Jones said a car pulled up outside his house, and the man ran across the road and jumped into the passenger seat. Because of the heavy rain, he pulled his jacket over his head, meaning Stan Jones couldn't get a good look at his face. The driver was a young woman with long, dark hair, but Mr Jones could only guess her age was between eighteen and thirty."

"I don't suppose he got a registration?" asked Gus.

Kenneth Truelove shook his head. Gus Freeman sighed.

"Nobody said it was going to be easy," said Geoff Mercer.

"What about the marriage?" asked Gus.

"They had only been married for six months, Gus," said Geoff. "They had hardly had time to recover from the honeymoon."

"I didn't mean Richard and Eve Chaloner," said Gus. "I meant her first marriage."

"Eve was married to John Allsopp for fourteen years," said Kenneth. "The couple lived in Westbury after they married in 2000 and moved to Warminster in 2008. John Allsopp began an affair with a younger woman from work after a Christmas party at the end of 2013. Eve wasn't the forgiving type, and the marriage ended. She moved to Swindon, bumped into Richard Chaloner in a bar in the town centre, and married within a year. As Geoff suggested, they were as happy as pigs in the proverbial. John Allsopp and the young woman had split up even before the decree absolute. He still lives and works in Warminster, and his alibi was solid for the time of the murder. Allsopp was aware Eve had moved to Swindon, but there was no evidence to suggest he knew Eve had remarried. Unless he fooled DS Spencer when he interviewed him, John Allsopp didn't have means, motive, or opportunity to murder Richard Chaloner."

"Let's try another angle then," said Gus. "I'm fed up with dead-ends. Was there any reason Chaloner hadn't married until he reached the age of forty-four? Did he have any other serious relationships? Was he hiding a secret from his new wife, perhaps? Had Richard Chaloner ever been in trouble with the law? If he'd been in prison for ten to fifteen years, that would have reduced his chances of wedded bliss."

"Chaloner didn't have a record, Gus," said Geoff.

"According to the case file, Richard Chaloner had never been in a serious relationship," said Kenneth. "He wasn't a keen sportsperson, but he'd joined various clubs and societies over the years. His friends and family described him as gregarious. It certainly wasn't the case that Chaloner was a loner, far from it. From everything I can see in this file, he spent his twenties and thirties working hard and enjoying his leisure time with a wide circle of friends."

"He wasn't happy to settle for second-best," said Geoff Mercer. "I think the reputation his business had earned was evidence of that."

"Chaloner acted quickly enough when the right woman came into his life," said Kenneth. "The couple had much to look forward to, but someone stole that dream."

"Another dead end," said Gus. "I can see why Sengupta and Spencer initially thought they were dealing with a straightforward robbery. It would be easy to imagine an attack coming from a junkie hoping to score enough money to satisfy his craving. A quick in-and-out to collect cash and a bank card by waving a knife or machete at a frightened business owner. A robbery that offered the opportunity for a few hundred pounds would be common enough in a large town like Swindon, but this smells different. Guns are more available these days, but the mere threat of violence is often enough to get a shop owner to open the till. In this instance, the intruder didn't panic after he'd shot Richard Chaloner."

"What are you saying, Freeman?" asked the Chief Constable.

"He'd done his homework; that was obvious," said Gus. "He knew Harry Simpkins always left at five-thirty. Matt Merchant's car was outside until ten to six. If he'd studied the men's routine over weeks, he knew Merchant needed it to drive somewhere other than his house on Elmina Road on Monday evenings."

"Surely the killer must have panicked when Merchant spotted the puncture, Gus," said Geoff. "What if Matt Merchant had persuaded Chaloner to accept a lift? The opportunity to rob Chaloner would have gone."

"If I'm right, and the killer made meticulous preparations, he knew how insistent Chaloner would be on cycling to and from work. He'd cycled every day from Pinehurst before he married, and nothing changed afterwards. Chaloner needed to repair the tyre somewhen, and the killer played the odds. He gambled Chaloner would politely decline the offer of a lift, stay behind to finish the paperwork, make the repair, and then cycle home to Shrivenham Road. His wife was on holiday, so nobody was waiting for him to get home. The weather was another factor to play into the hands of the killer. If Chaloner took the opportunity to hang around indoors for another thirty minutes, the downpour could have eased."

"If we accept that's what happened before the attack,

talk us through events inside the garage, Freeman," said Kenneth.

"Where was Chaloner when Merchant left?" asked Gus.

"Merchant fetched him from the office after he'd spotted the damage to the bicycle," said Geoff.

"The autopsy report states the body hadn't been moved," said Gus. "Chaloner was shot at close range in the middle of the workshop floor. Simpkins and Merchant found him the following morning lying between two cars. There were no signs of any struggle anywhere on the premises."

"The intruder persuaded Chaloner to leave the office," said Geoff.

"The cash was said to be in his wallet," said Gus. "Where was the wallet found?"

Kenneth Truelove scanned the report.

"On the floor, just outside the office door. It got kicked under a workbench."

"Merchant said it was common for the bank card to be lying on the desk," said Gus. "Chaloner might have kept his wallet in the back pocket of his trousers, but when you spend your working life under the bonnet of a car, it's usual to protect your clothing. The photographs of the murder scene confirm Chaloner was indeed wearing a blue boiler-suit with zipped pockets at the front and his day-to-day clothing underneath. In addition, photographs of the office show a pair of shoes he would change into when cycling home, a jacket, and wet-weather gear. Once he'd repaired the bike, Chaloner would have changed out of his boiler suit and work boots and cycled home."

"You think the wallet was in the inside pocket of the jacket in the office?" asked Geoff.

"That's why you believe the killer kept his cool and didn't panic," said Kenneth.

"I think he waited for Matt Merchant to drive away, walked through the side door, switched off the lights, and made for the centre of the garage. Richard Chaloner went to investigate. He probably thought it was kids messing around or an opportunist thief hoping to grab a valuable piece of kit and escape before Chaloner caught him. He had no idea the intruder aimed to murder him in cold blood."

"So, the killer waited in the dark until Chaloner got close and shot him," said Geoff.

"Do you not think there was an argument, Freeman?" asked Kenneth.

"There were no signs of a struggle. The killer coolly removed the gold chain, stepped over the body, strolled to the office, and helped himself to the cash. If Chaloner had the wallet on his person, the CSI personnel would have noted any disturbance to his clothing. The killer removed Chaloner's gold chain without leaving evidence, which supports the view they wore gloves. The bank card was a bonus, but they had ample time to look around the office, find the PIN, and add the four hundred pounds to whatever was in the wallet to cement the idea it was a robbery."

"How do you explain the thefts of the catalytic converters?" asked Geoff Mercer.

"At some point, Sengupta and Spencer linked the killing to the CCTV caper you made me sit through," said Gus. "Am I right?"

"That didn't happen until they had exhausted the other lines of enquiry," said Kenneth.

"My initial thoughts are that the two events were unconnected," said Gus.

"The team spent a long time trying to find the men responsible," said the Chief Constable. "They hunted for evidence linking Chaloner with the criminal fraternity."

"Without luck, I imagine?" asked Gus.

"I wouldn't be asking you to take a fresh look at the case if they had, Freeman."

"We'll check everything, sir, as we always do," said Gus, "but my guess is the killer was local. We're looking for someone who could keep watch on the garage without attracting attention. Mrs Fryer and Mr Jones would have spotted a stranger spending long periods on the street outside their window. The killer was someone they knew. He may well have been someone Richard Chaloner knew."

"You haven't had the file in your hand for thirty minutes, and you believe you're on the verge of solving it," said Geoff Mercer. "Have you got a bus to catch?"

"I thought you would be on the same page as me by now, Geoff," said Gus. "This wasn't a robbery gone wrong, nor does it feel like an argument over money for stolen goods. As for solving it, we're a long way from doing that. It is, however, imperative we catch this killer. How he behaved after the shooting suggests that Richard Chaloner wasn't his first victim."

Chapter Three

"LET'S not jump to conclusions, Freeman," said the Chief Constable. "Raj Sengupta might not be the brightest star in the heavens, but surely someone on his team imagined the same sequence of events you've hypothesised. Moreover, as the team switched focus to the catalytic converter thefts, it suggests they found a good reason to discount your theory."

"You need to read this murder file in more detail, Gus," agreed Geoff Mercer. "If you were right, the killer struck again in the past two years. However, the streets near Swindon railway station have shown no sign of being home to a serial killer."

"You might be right," said Gus. "We'll follow the evidence Raj and Tom uncovered. They never found the link to organised crime, but that doesn't mean it wasn't there. Similarly, they never identified the three men seen in the garage's vicinity on the day of the murder. Whether that was unlucky or sloppy police work, we'll only discover by going over everything with a fine-tooth comb."

"An open mind, Freeman," said Kenneth. "That's all I can ask."

While Gus flicked through the appendices at the back of the file, Kenneth Truelove called Vera Butler and asked her to serve lunch.

Geoff Mercer leaned forward to speak to Gus.

"Has Suzie told you I'd asked her to run a campaign encouraging car owners to be more careful in protecting their valuables?"

"Yes, Geoff," said Gus. "Only a few weeks ago, you added hate crimes and victim support to her list of the latest hot potatoes. Can't someone have a quiet word with the Police and Crime Commissioner? Too many carbohydrates aren't good for you."

"The PCC aims to deliver an effective and efficient service, Gus. When he says jump, we jump. It stops him from looking in our direction when he's looking for further reductions in personnel. I'm only following orders from Kenneth. Has Suzie complained?"

"Not yet," said Gus, thinking ahead to next Tuesday's visit to the doctor.

There was a knock at the door. Vera and Kassie each wheeled in a trolley laden with today's goodies. Enough to feed a small army, let alone three people.

"I see you ordered the usual, Geoff," said Gus. "No signs of any reduction there."

"Don't worry, Mr Freeman," said Kassie as she paused by his chair. "I added your favourite to the order we submitted to the suppliers."

Gus accepted the proffered bacon roll and kept watch on a healthy-looking wrap. It was unlikely Geoff Mercer would grab it, but stranger things had happened.

He glanced again at the Richard Chaloner murder file

lying on Kenneth's desk. Had he jumped too soon? Where would they need to look for the missing link between the garage owner and the people behind the car thieves from that CCTV footage?

"I'll see you when you've finished your lunch, Mr Freeman," whispered Kassie as she wheeled her trolley towards the door.

"Have you had any further fanciful thoughts now you've demolished that bacon roll, Freeman?" asked Kenneth.

"Did the Gablecross detectives explore every avenue, sir? I've only skimmed the file's contents, but I couldn't see any reference to enemies Richard Chaloner made during his twenty-odd years in the garage trade. On the contrary, his two employees painted a picture of a splendid chap who went the extra mile for each of his clients. It was a pleasure to go to work every day. Yet Chaloner gave short shrift to the unscheduled visitor they had that morning. Why didn't Chaloner take fifteen minutes out of his busy day to check the intermittent electrical fault? It could have been an easy fix, and he would have gained another potential repeat customer."

"DI Sengupta didn't find anyone who had a bad word to say about Chaloner," said Kenneth.

"Each of us has collared dozens of rogues whose friends and family swore were as pure as the driven snow," said Gus, "and several of them have worked in this very business."

"I admit rogues exist in the motor trade, Gus," said Geoff Mercer. "Dodgy workshops in the back streets where they issue MOTs for vehicles that should never be on the road. The owner dressed in oily overalls, manually rewinding the mileage with a screwdriver. Many think that practice died with the demise of analogue. The reality is that instead of being a modern, secure solution, the digital versions have made it easier for a vehicle's apparent mileage to get altered."

Gus wondered whether his old Ford Focus had ever suffered the fate of getting clocked. It didn't seem likely. Every mile his Focus had travelled was etched into its daily performance.

"Although the practice hasn't disappeared, surely it's rarer than in the old days?"

"Clocking is on the increase," said Kenneth. He searched through the pile of reports on his desk.

"Have you read every one of those reports, sir?" asked Gus.

"I'm obliged to pay attention to trends, Freeman," said Kenneth. The seventh file down was the one he sought. "Two years ago, one in twenty cars in the UK showed a discrepancy between the actual and apparent mileage displayed. That has increased to one in sixteen. As a result, the potential cost to motorists has risen to around eight hundred million pounds every year."

"A not inconsiderable sum," said Geoff.

"A sum caused by the impact on second-hand values," said Gus. "Yes, I understand the maths. My Ford Focus has done over one hundred thousand miles. If I took it to one of these dodgy operators and they knocked forty thousand miles off the milometer, I might get an extra two thousand pounds if I was to sell it."

"Chaloner wasn't a second-hand car dealer," said Kenneth. "He only carried out repairs and MOTs. There's no suggestion he ever had a car for sale on the forecourt outside his garage."

"True," said Geoff, "but he must have had customers bringing cars to him for their first MOT after three years on the road. So I think Gus is right to pursue another line of enquiry."

"Ah," said the Chief Constable. "You're pointing fingers at the car owners, not the garage owners. That's because of PCP, the most popular method of purchasing cars in the UK in recent years."

"Exactly," said Geoff. "Finance deals for personal contract purchase, or hire, often come with strict mileage limits, where each additional mile can prove costly. If you say you're only going to do five thousand miles per year on a three-year deal and cover double the distance, it could cost you fifteen hundred quid."

"My car needs servicing each year to get it through the MOT," said Gus, "and has its mileage recorded in the service book."

"Yes, but did you buy that rust bucket from new?" asked Geoff.

"Keep your voice down; she might hear you," said Gus. "Yes, I did, but although I didn't need to pass an MOT, I still got it checked over, and they recorded the mileage."

"Many drivers don't bother visiting a garage until that first MOT is due. It's easy to get a car clocked before it goes to the garage."

"That's illegal," said Gus.

"It's illegal to alter the mileage and then sell a car without telling the buyer its mileage has changed," said Geoff. "The act of turning back the clock isn't illegal."

"If Richard Chaloner got involved in that business, what equipment did he need?" asked Gus. "The days of the screwdriver are long gone, I presume?"

"Just a laptop and software available online," said Geoff. "If he didn't fancy doing the job himself, he could arrange for someone to pop in and do it for one hundred pounds."

"We'll check with Merchant and Simpkins," said Gus. "What happened to the garage after Chaloner's death?"

"Merchant has continued running the business, trading under Merchant Motor Repairs," said Kenneth. "Harry Simpkins is still there, and they now have a young apprentice motor mechanic, Anne Marie Buckland. Chaloner's widow, Eve, was happy to let Merchant take over the unit's rental. She lives alone in the house the couple shared for six months on Shrivenham Road."

"As this murder occurred only two years ago, almost every person Sengupta and Spencer interviewed is living and working where they were at the time," said Geoff Mercer. "Even the CCTV footage came from the same postal district next to the railway station. So if the killer were local, you wouldn't have far to look, Gus."

"We'll see," said Gus. "Is that it for today, sir?"

"I need to attend another briefing in ten minutes, Freeman," said Kenneth. "I would welcome the opportunity to spend that brief respite in quiet contemplation."

"Message received, sir," said Gus. "I'll rescue that chicken wrap and get this folder back to the Crime Review Team office."

Geoff Mercer took his cue from Gus, and they both headed for the door. As Gus held it open for his colleague, he spotted the Chief Constable standing by his window. With responsibility comes sacrifice. The view from that window wasn't a patch on the one Geoff Mercer now enjoyed. So far, the PCC had resisted the temptation to include his pal in the bloated ranks of Assistant Chief Constables, for which both Gus and Geoff would be eternally grateful.

"I'll monitor Suzie's workload, Gus," said Geoff when they were outside. "I'd hate for her to buckle under the strain. She's a safe pair of hands. When I look around my team for the right person for the job, Suzie stands head and shoulders above the rest."

"I understand your problem, Geoff," said Gus. "Suzie relishes the opportunity of sticking her head above the parapet. She's ambitious, and apart from being taller than you, Suzie reminds me of what you were like in your youth."

"You never change, you cheeky beggar," said Geoff. "Don't forget what Kenneth said about looking after Blessing. Take one of the three lads with you when you interview someone. It's for their benefit as much as for you. Good luck with the case; I fancy you'll need it."

Geoff walked the short distance to his office, and Gus looked across the administration area for signs of Vera or Kassie.

"Has your meeting with the Chief Constable finished?"

Gus recognised the icy tones of Ms Packenham.

"When I was holidaying in the Balearics with my late wife many years ago, we watched a group of young women dancing. They wore a traditional costume, with long black skirts that kissed the ground. The way they circled the musicians suggested they were on roller skates rather than the balls of their feet. It was fascinating, and whatever they were doing under those skirts made no discernible sound. You achieved the same result in trousers and sensible lace-up shoes. I'm impressed."

"You didn't answer my question," said Grace Packenham.

"You didn't explain why you needed to know," said Gus. "I answer to DS Mercer. If he wishes me to leave the London Road offices within one minute of the conclusion of a meeting, he'll instruct me through the proper channels. Have you had your regulation thirty-minute break today,

Ms Packenham? That looks like mayonnaise on your shirt. Perhaps you should be in your office, not chatting here with me. Your productivity ratio is suffering."

Grace opened her mouth to speak, but Gus turned on his heel and headed for a green flash he'd spotted on the other side of the office. Kassie Trotter was closing in on the filing cabinets she'd pointed to earlier. He wanted to collect his slice of summer berry cake and escape without further delay.

"Am I in trouble again, Mr Freeman," asked Kassie. "She's always on my case, that one."

"Keep your head down and ignore her," said Gus.

"Ms Misery has gone to her office, Mr Freeman. We're in the clear."

Kassie handed over Gus's afternoon treat.

"Is that a chicken wrap, Mr Freeman? Are you still hungry?"

"The Chief Constable was in a hurry to get us out of his office, Kassie. I don't enjoy seeing food go to waste. Give my regards to Vera. I'll see you next Monday, if not before."

Gus was soon downstairs and outside the building. The sun was high in the sky, and his Focus was an oven. There was nothing for it. He had to risk opening the windows. As he drove back to the Old Police Station office, he thought it might require a trip to Merchant Motor Repairs if the windows refused to return to their normal position.

Thirty minutes later, Gus arrived in the car park below the Crime Review Team office. He breathed a sigh of relief as his windows closed as instructed. He collected the folder and his two treats from the passenger seat and walked to the lift door.

"That sounded like someone called the lift," said Neil a few seconds later.

"We'd better make it look as if we've been working," said Lydia.

"I wonder whose murder we've got this time," said Blessing.

Gus emerged from the lift and saw five faces staring at what he was carrying.

"I didn't have time to finish lunch," he said, "and Kassie Trotter baked a cake at the weekend. Although, I don't know why I should explain myself."

"You've got the new case folder, guv," said Lydia. "That's what we were looking for."

"Two years ago, in Swindon, someone shot a garage owner," said Gus. "The killer stole cash and a bank card, but I don't think robbery was the motive."

"Who was the victim, guv?" asked Luke.

"Where did the killing take place?" asked Alex.

"The victim was forty-four-year-old Richard Chaloner, and his garage was half a mile from Swindon station."

"We've already got street maps for that part of town, guv," said Lydia. "I'll get them onto the wall."

"Can I delve into the murder file, guv?" asked Blessing. "You'll want the crime scene photos on the whiteboard."

Gus dropped the file on Lydia's desk and put his wrap and slice of cake into his desk drawer for safekeeping. Lydia distributed the copies of the summary sheets to the others.

"Who was in charge of the investigation, guv?" asked Luke.

"DI Sengupta was Senior Investigating Officer, and his second-in-command was DS Tom Spencer. So the murder fell into the lap of detectives at Gablecross, as you would expect."

"Who do we want to interview first, guv," asked Neil. "Was the victim married?"

"He was," said Gus. "Richard and Eve Chaloner had only been married for six months at the time of the murder. Chaloner was a bachelor; his wife had been married before. The details are in the folder. Who would you want to speak to first, Neil?"

"That could be a trick question, guv," said Neil. "I can give my mate, Jake Latimer a call, to get the lowdown on how they handled the case. If it was a mess, then it might be best to speak to the wife first. But hang on, you haven't told us whether this garage was a one-person outfit or one of the big boys. How many people did Chaloner employ?"

"Just two, Neil," said Gus. "Matt Merchant, twenty-nine, and Harry Simpkins, sixty-one. Merchant runs the business these days. Simpkins assists him, and there's an apprentice. They operate out of a unit on a side street near the station."

"That street has an effective Neighbourhood Watch, guv," said Alex. "They spotted three strangers in the garage's vicinity during the day of the murder. I wonder why the detectives couldn't name any of them?"

"We can try a fresh approach, Alex," said Gus. "The first person spotted was driving a white van. He wore white overalls. I want to find whoever DS Spencer spoke to and push them for more details. Do you remember Raj Sengupta? He reported to Jack Sanders on the Stacey Read investigation. We can talk to him at Gablecross whenever we wish. He's head of the cybercrime unit these days and permanently indoors. I don't know what Tom Spencer's working on, but it's only two years, so maybe nothing's changed, and he's grafting as a Detective Sergeant. The boss told me Tom Spencer did the heavy work on the investigation. Raj sat in his office dreaming up strategies."

"It sounds as if I should call Jake, guv," said Neil.

"It won't do any harm, Neil," said Gus.

"How do you propose finding white van man, guv?" asked Lydia.

"We'll need more detail on the van. Whether there was signage identifying the firm for which he worked. It's odds-on the guy was self-employed, but only a handful of occupations use white overalls day-to-day. My guess is he's a painter and decorator with his own business, but I'm prepared to be proved wrong. Once we add more details to this original murder file, I'd search trade directories, either in print or online. One of them will find us this person. We need to speak to him and either put him in the frame or drop him from our enquiries."

"They had little to go on to identify the young man stood outside Mrs Fryer's house, guv," said Blessing. "He could be anybody. There wasn't a connection to the garage as there had been for the other two persons of interest. He didn't cross the road. The eyewitness couldn't categorically state he was even interested in the garage. He could have been waiting for someone or was unemployed and had nothing better to do than hang around on a street corner."

"Blessing's right, guv," said Lydia. "We've got zero chance of identifying him, and he didn't enter the garage or stare through the window. Mr Jones wanted to be helpful with the third person of interest, but his description of the man and woman was vague. I wonder whether Mrs Fryer caught sight of those two. There's no mention of the Afro-Caribbean chap and his girlfriend in DS Spencer's interview. He only took notes for Mrs Fryer's sighting of the youngster stood outside her house."

"Good point, Lydia," said Gus. "That's something we can ask. Mrs Fryer worked a morning shift at a care home, which meant she didn't see the white van and its driver.

Stan Jones may have done. I imagine he spends much of his time indoors. Check the murder file to see if Spencer followed up on what he'd heard about the argument in the morning. Perhaps he missed something from the house-to-house enquiries the uniformed officers carried out. You had better add a question regarding the young man outside Mrs Fryer's place while you're at it. He may have walked past Stan Jones's house to get to the spot where he stood, waiting, or watching."

The office was a hive of activity for the next hour as the team dissected the murder file. They posted street maps, crime scene photos, and a list of the main characters in the drama. Luke was preparing a running order for the interviews for Gus to consider. He never got it right the first time, but Gus didn't enjoy staring at a blank sheet of paper.

"Who wants to go first?" asked Gus. "Give me your first impressions."

"Based on your observation when you entered the office, guv," said Neil, "you don't think it was a robbery. You haven't yet explained why. If I hadn't heard that comment, I'd say this was a classic case of a young thug, armed with a gun, bursting into the garage after the others had left. He threatened Chaloner, who handed over the cash from his wallet, and the gold chain. Something spooked the attacker. Maybe Chaloner tried to distract him and grabbed for the gun. The autopsy showed the gunman was only three feet away from the victim. The thug may not have intended to kill Chaloner."

"You think the attacker was an addict desperate for cash for his next fix?" asked Gus.

"The wallet contained less than one hundred pounds," said Lydia, "and that solved his problem in the short term.

He could have flogged the gold chain in a pub. It doesn't fit with the bank card, though."

"Why not?" asked Neil. "Chaloner was lying on the floor, dead or dying. His attacker searched the garage for items easily disposed of for cash to add to his haul. It wasn't a huge unit, only enough floor space for two vehicles, side by side. The office was a likely spot for a mobile phone or a laptop. I reckon he couldn't believe his luck when he spotted the bank card on the desk. How long would it have taken him to rummage through a few drawers and paperwork on the desk, hunting for a record of the PIN? A minute, tops. He spotted a scrap of paper pinned to the board on the wall, realised what it was, forgot everything else, and got out. Why run off with bulky items that only yield a small return when he was guaranteed a cash pay-out at an ATM?"

"The young thugs you're describing aren't cool and calculating, Neil," said Alex. "I could imagine the panic he experienced if the gun went off accidentally. He would have scarpered without giving the office, or anywhere else in the garage, a second thought."

"What do you think happened, Alex?" asked Gus.

"Chaloner didn't have any enemies, guv, according to people Tom Spencer interviewed. I know Tom from my days at Gablecross. He's methodical. So, whatever path Raj Sengupta determined they should follow, Tom would have stuck to it. Raj decided it was a robbery, so Tom looked for a likely candidate."

"Tunnel vision," said Luke. "He tried to find that young white man stood across the road and the Afro-Caribbean guy peering through the window later in the afternoon. Their actions play into the idea it was a robbery. One, or both, men wanted to learn everything they could of the layout inside the garage, check on how many people they needed to see leave at the end of the working day. The attacker didn't leave evidence at the scene, and there were no signs of a struggle. So why couldn't there have been two men inside the garage? One man searching the office while the other handled Chaloner. Neil's suggestion might not be that wide of the mark, guv. Two men working in tandem could explain Alex's reservations over the lack of panic."

"So, you think it could have been a robbery, Luke?" asked Gus.

"As Neil said, you haven't told us what convinced you it wasn't," said Luke.

"Try to be patient for a while longer, Luke. I haven't heard from either of the ladies yet."

Blessing was sitting closest to the whiteboard where she had posted the crime scene photos.

"Richard Chaloner was wearing one of those all-in-one outfits, with a zip from the neck to below the waist, guv. It protected his normal clothes from getting covered with muck. Look at the photos. He didn't stuff his breast pockets with small tools or personal items. Where was his wallet? If it was in the office, why was the body found lying in the middle of the floor? The young thug Neil described would have burst in through the side door waving the gun, shouting. Chaloner was working in the office to the right, according to Matt Merchant. The thug could have got the money, the chain, and the bank card without leaving the room. Why shoot Chaloner? The attacker had cash and something to sell, but at some point, he made Chaloner walk into the workshop area. Either Neil's scenario played out, and the gun went off by accident, or the thug lost patience with Chaloner and gunned him down."

"There was no evidence to suggest the attacker tortured Chaloner," said Gus.

"Whether or not Chaloner gave the attacker the PIN, it didn't alter the outcome, guv," said Lydia. "We can't know why the attack ended in murder. The attacker could have been wearing a ski mask. He might have had just a scarf around the lower half of his face or no disguise. If it was one desperate man acting alone, he could have got everything he went there for and suddenly realised he needed to kill Chaloner."

"Chaloner could have recognised his attacker, guv," said Blessing. "Or it dawned on the attacker that Chaloner could give the police a decent description. But, as Alex pointed out, the type of criminal who carries out these opportunist crimes isn't the brightest spark."

Gus checked his computer. Good news. Kenneth Truelove had sent through a copy of the CCTV footage they had viewed at London Road. Perhaps that would sow seeds of doubt in the younger minds sat in front of him.

"I'll upload this information to the Freeman Files so we can watch it together," he said. "This theft took place several days before Richard Chaloner died."

The team sat in silence and watched the two thieves calmly stealing the catalytic converter.

"They knew what they were doing, didn't they," said Alex. "They were back inside the van inside two minutes; job done."

"They drove a white van," said Neil. "Is that significant, guv?"

"The number plate belonged to a VW Passat, stolen from Membury service station on the M4, seven weeks earlier," said Gus. "We could take photos of the van and the two men back to people canvassed in the house-to-house. We definitely need to show them to the person who told Tom Spencer about the man in white overalls arguing with Chaloner at eleven in the morning. Whether it was the same white van, who knows?

"Both men were white," said Blessing. "That doesn't fit with the idea the young man stood outside Mrs Fryer's house was working with the coloured guy seen later in the day."

"True, Blessing," said Gus, "but what made the Gable-cross team think the events were ever related?"

"Catalytic converters are worth a small fortune," said Luke. "That had attracted the interest of organised crime gangs, and as usual, they refined the process into a slick operation."

"They separate the converters containing precious metals from the car owners," said Neil, "and divert them to scrap dealers who don't ask questions."

"I recognise those buildings, guv," said Alex. "That's a couple of streets away from the station."

"I know that district too," said Neil. "I reckon that's Henry Street."

"How far is that from the railway station?" asked Blessing.

"A two-minute drive," said Neil.

"Chaloner's two employees lived nearby," said Lydia. "Which road is the garage on?"

"Ponting Street," said Luke. "Most of the housing by the railway station sprung up thanks to Isambard Kingdom Brunel. If he'd selected another town as a staging post along his Great Western Railway, Swindon would have remained an isolated market town, as it was in the days of the stage-coach. After God's Wonderful Railway arrived, they opened the Railway Works in 1843 as a repair and maintenance facility. Sixty years later, the engineering works had expanded to employ over twelve thousand people, all of whom needed housing. There are dozens of streets of Victorian terraced houses to the south of the station."

"What does the proximity of the theft to Chaloner's garage suggest?" asked Gus.

"I've read nothing in the murder file to suggest Richard Chaloner was a criminal, guv," said Blessing.

"If we can take the statements given by his employees and his customers as gospel, then Chaloner was as honest as the day is long," said Alex.

"Did Raj Sengupta and Tom Spencer switch horses, guv?" asked Neil. "They had no joy identifying the three persons of interest and couldn't find anyone with a grudge against Chaloner. So they started looking for links with something dodgy."

"If he got involved with an organised crime gang," said Lydia, "you could understand how Chaloner would end up as he did if he crossed them. Was that what you thought, guv? Is that why you believed this wasn't a straightforward robbery?"

"The Chief Constable thought I was hasty in my conclusion that there was something sinister about it," said Gus. "I deliberately didn't go into my thought processes in any detail until I heard what each of you thought."

"You held back the CCTV footage until we outlined our ideas based on the evidence we'd received," said Alex. "With the CCTV added into the mix, the picture looks very different. But, as Lydia said, if Chaloner was involved in either receiving stolen goods or helping a gang source the converters, that was something that could turn nasty, very quickly."

"Did Tom Spencer check that out, guv?" asked Neil.

"We need to delve deeper into the murder file to learn just how many leads the team followed, Neil," said Gus. "Safe to say, when the top brass at Gablecross pulled the plug on Sengupta's investigation, he and Spencer hadn't found a link between Chaloner and dodgy dealings."

"That doesn't mean it wasn't there," said Luke.

"That's word-for-word what I told the Chief Constable, Luke. So we'll take another look."

"If we found a link," said Blessing, "that could explain why Chaloner had to die. The robbery was to throw the police off the scent."

"That's a logical conclusion to draw, Blessing," said Lydia, "but Gus asked you why the Gablecross team thought the events were related."

"I've jumped in too soon," said Blessing.

"Each of us has been guilty of that at one time or another," grinned Gus.

"What am I missing, guv?" asked Blessing.

"I'm prepared to get shot down in flames," said Gus, "but nobody has mentioned the bicycle."

"The slashed tyre, guv?" asked Neil. "That was just a delaying tactic, surely, to keep Chaloner at the garage after Merchant and Simpkins went home. Everyone could have left at the same time if they hadn't done that. But, of course, Mrs Fryer wasn't watching the entire time that lad was standing outside her house. So perhaps he saw an opportunity to dash across and do the deed."

"Or Stan Jones could have missed that young woman, guv," said Luke. "Her partner was peering through the window, making sure everyone stayed indoors out of the rain, while she slashed the tyre. Then she ran back to the car and drove to collect him. So Stan Jones could have missed vital parts of the action unless he stood by the window full-time."

"I'm struggling to find a connection between organised crime gangs and bicycle tyres," said Gus.

"Gang members don't do subtle, is that what you're saying, guv?" asked Alex.

"It doesn't strike me as likely they would bother with the bicycle tyre. If Chaloner crossed them, or if he'd ripped them off, they would have gone in mob-handed. Guns are their stock-in-trade. The CSI team would have collected evidence that two or three men had visited the garage. There would have been much more damage. Enough to put Merchant and Simpkins out of a job and send a clear message to other garage owners they had their claws on."

"You're ruling out the possibility it was gang-related, guv?" said Neil.

"It's something we'll investigate with due diligence, Neil," said Gus. "However, I believe the answer lies in another direction. One thing that struck me was the lack of panic after he'd shot Richard Chaloner. The attacker had done his homework. He expected Harry Simpkins to leave at five-thirty on the dot. As for Merchant, if the attacker had kept watch for a time, he knew Monday nights differed from the other four nights of the week.

"Merchant played football on Mondays," said Lydia. "He was leaving at around ten to six to drive to Wootton Bassett but went back inside when he spotted the puncture. The attacker must have been watching when Chaloner and Merchant came outside to look."

"If Merchant had somewhere to be, he couldn't stay to help his boss or give him a lift home," said Luke. "That adds weight to your argument, guv, that the attack was well-planned."

"That was my thought earlier when I went through the case file with DS Mercer," said Gus. "Chaloner cycled to work every day of his working life. He wasn't about to abandon his bicycle for a mere puncture. So, after Merchant drove away, he returned to the office and his paperwork. According to the autopsy, the body hadn't been moved. Chaloner got shot at close range in the middle of the workshop floor. Simpkins and Merchant found him the following morning lying between two cars. There were no signs of any struggle anywhere on the premises. Which suggests the attacker somehow got Chaloner out of his office."

"I posed a question concerning the wallet earlier, guv," said Blessing. "I thought Chaloner would leave it in the office while he was working, not carry it in his pocket throughout the day. He didn't need it, did he? So, to steal the cash, the attacker had to go to the office first, surely?"

"The wallet was found under a workbench by the office door," said Gus. "There's a photo in the appendix towards the back of the file."

"So the attacker took the money, threw away the wallet, and forced Chaloner into the workshop to kill him," said Lydia. "Why?"

"Why did he kill him, or why take him to the workshop?" asked Neil.

"Run through the sequence of events once more," said Gus.

"The bank card was lying on the desk," said Luke. "The attacker could have taken the cash, gold chain, and bank card within the first minute of walking through the side door. Of course, it could have taken longer to get the PIN information out of Chaloner, but it had to be over quickly."

"Why?" asked Gus.

"The confirmed time of death was between six and seven, guv," said Luke.

"When you enter through a door situated two-thirds along the side of a building, how many options do you have?" asked Gus.

"Left, right, and straight ahead," said Neil. "Unless you're in the wrong building."

"I think after Matt Merchant drove away, the attacker walked through the side door, switched off the lights, walked to his left past the first car, and crossed to the centre of the garage. Richard Chaloner left the office to investigate, and as soon as he got close enough, the killer shot him. That explains why there were no signs of a struggle. The killer now had plenty of time to remove the gold chain from around Chaloner's neck and find other items to add to the illusion this was a robbery. Chaloner's wallet was probably in his jacket pocket. The bank card was on the desk, and thanks to a stroke of luck, the killer spotted the PIN on the noticeboard. He switched off the workshop lights, closed the door behind him, and left."

"Why didn't he switch off the office lights?" asked Lydia.

"I can't be certain he never went inside the garage before that night, but I suspect he thought the switches by the door extinguished all the lights. He wasn't daft enough to wander back inside just to rectify that slip. The dog walkers would be on the streets within minutes. Someone could have recognised him."

"You think the killer was local, guv?" asked Neil.

"That's my guess, Neil," said Gus. "We're looking for someone who could keep watch on the garage without attracting attention. The nosy neighbours would have spotted a stranger spending long periods on the street outside their window. So the killer was someone they didn't have any concerns about seeing on Ponting Street."

"This wasn't a robbery gone wrong, guv, was it?" said Alex.

"We've almost ruled out the possibility it was gang-related," said Luke.

"What does that leave us with?" asked Gus.

"A mystery within a mystery," said Blessing Umeh.

Chapter Four

GUS LEFT the office at five o'clock to drive home to the bungalow. The preliminary discussions on the Chaloner murder had taken longer than expected. It wasn't straightforward, that was certain; there was much to do.

In his haste to get home to Suzie, he'd left the wrap and slice of cake in the desk drawer. Kassie Trotter's summer berry cake would survive the night, but the healthy wrap would already be wilting. You can't win them all.

Gus spotted the Reverend's bicycle as he drove past the entrance to the allotments. He hadn't seen her or Brett at the weekend, so he stopped for a chat.

Clemency Bentham was another who was wilting in the heat.

"I know what you're thinking, Gus," she said. "The afternoon sun has caused this hot flush. Despite the number of pounds I've shed, two hours of gardening in the heat of the afternoon takes it out of one. I blame you, of course. Your patch is a picture these days. You put me to shame."

"Suzie and I were here twice over last weekend," said

Gus. "I recognised I needed to do something drastic to catch up with Bert Penman. I'd stayed away too long. We kept missing one another. How are you both?"

"Bert was here before lunch," said Clemency. "He left the Crown just after I arrived. I imagine he had a liquid lunch and slept it off in his orchard this afternoon."

"I meant you and Brett," said Gus. "I tend to think of you as a couple, or am I wrong?"

"Of course not, Gus. I'm happy for my parishioners and other villagers to see us as a couple. We have to observe certain standards, of course."

"Brett can't leave the vicarage first thing in the morning," said Gus. "Yes, I can see that wouldn't go down well with the Bishop or the less tolerant locals."

"That isn't an issue at this stage," said Clemency, blushing even more than Gus thought possible. "Not that it's anyone's business."

"I didn't mean to pry," said Gus, wishing the ground would open and swallow him. "How's Brett's work at the vet's going? Are they busy?"

"Every day is different, Gus. Brett tells me that on Friday, he left home at half-past eight to drive to Wootton Bassett," said the Reverend. "His first job was to visit the kennels to see if any new patients got booked in by the duty vet overnight. Next, he received an update on the in-patients from one of the veterinary nurses and decided which needed immediate attention. When he'd cleared that list, he reached his consulting room and called the first patient of the day. Last Friday, he had a rabbit with a painful abdomen, a dog with pancreatitis who was vomiting and looked dehydrated."

"Charming," said Gus. "Does Brett get a break for lunch?"

"It was nowhere near lunchtime when that happened, Gus," laughed Clemency. "Brett says the surgery is fully booked, with ten-minute appointments throughout the morning. He deals with vaccinations, minor problems, and routine health checks on a range of small animals. While he's engaged in that part of the job, his support staff take pre-op blood and give pre-medications to get his surgery patients nice and relaxed for their procedures. Then, after a brief break for a quick coffee and a sandwich, he was spaying, castrating, removing a large bladder stone, and carrying out dental work on patients for over three hours. Finally, he arrived home at five-thirty, fell asleep in the chair, and called me at eight to apologise for not picking me up at seven. We had arranged to visit the Wharf Theatre in Devizes to watch a Youth Workshop production."

"Will you be able to keep Brett awake this evening?" asked Gus. "I don't know what Suzie wants to do yet, but this spell of hot weather encourages me to spend an evening in the Crown's beer garden."

"I'll ask Brett when I speak to him," said the Reverend. "We hadn't made plans. But, looking at that church clock, I'd better get back to the vicarage. If he's home already, I could miss his call."

"I haven't heard Suzie's Golf roar past the gateway," said Gus. "She tries to leave work by half-past five, but DS Mercer has given her even more work to handle."

"Suzie looks well on it, Gus," said Clemency. "Perhaps cutting out the alcohol is having health benefits."

Gus thought it wise not to comment. Next Tuesday wasn't that far away.

Clemency retrieved her bicycle, and after adjusting the strap on her bonnet, she set out along the lane towards the vicarage.

"We may see you later, Gus," she called over her shoulder. "No promises."

Gus allowed the Reverend time to get past the Crown before driving to the bungalow. As he inched out of the gateway, Suzie's car appeared from the left, and she tooted her horn as she passed by. They turned off the lane together and parked under the neatly arranged yellow roses on the side of their home.

"Did you finish early?" she asked.

"Not today," said Gus. "I spotted the Reverend's bicycle and stopped for a chat. She hoped to persuade Brett to join her in the beer garden later. What do you think?"

"It sounds good to me," said Suzie. "It's too hot to cook. How did things go today?"

"Kenneth handed us a new case. Only two years old this time. Do you remember the Richard Chaloner murder?"

"The man shot in his garage in Swindon. I can remember it, but nobody at London Road had much involvement. The Hub was still in the planning stages, and Gablecross felt confident they could get a result with the team they picked."

"They didn't get far in the time allowed to them," said Gus.

"No doubt they got dragged away after five or six weeks to tackle something more likely to get a result," said Suzie.

"It sounds like you've had a tough day," Gus said.

"Too many plates to keep spinning, Gus," she sighed. "Results are the only thing that matters these days."

They went inside the bungalow, and Gus sifted through the mail while Suzie had a shower. He gained a degree of satisfaction from throwing his two unsolicited invitations to buy something he'd never use into the recycling bin. There seemed little point to the postal service these days, as most items were junk mail. Gus placed Suzie's letters on the hall table.

"All yours," she said as she left the bathroom minutes later.

Suzie carried on into their bedroom while Gus took his turn in the shower. When he came out five minutes later, Suzie was standing in the hallway with one of her letters.

"Something interesting?" he asked.

"Get dressed, Gus," she said. "Nothing to worry you."

Gus put on a short-sleeved shirt and slacks. When he returned to the hallway, Suzie stood by the door, ready to leave for the pub.

"I don't think Brett and Clemency will get there for another hour, at least," he said. "What's the rush?"

"I need a drink," said Suzie. "You've got between here and the Crown to persuade me not to drink an entire bottle of Chardonnay."

"You said your letter was nothing to worry me," said Gus. "I'm worried now."

"It's Vicky. She's in hospital. The letter was from one of her colleagues. You know Vicky's paranoia about people finding out she was working with me. Last week, she got a single mum with two young children into a refuge. Her partner had physically and psychologically abused her and the kids for months. Vicky persuaded the woman to walk away from the relationship and stay with her parents over the weekend. The partner constantly phoned her, shouting threats and cursing her parents. Nobody in the house felt safe. Finally, last Monday morning, Vicky moved the wife and children to a place of safety. The partner must have seen a reference to Vicky in the local press. The PCC had given interviews championing the association between the Police and Victim

Support. Press reports mentioned my name, showed my photograph and used the quotes I'd made to the reporter."

"You met Vicky last Monday morning," said Gus. "You told me how nervous she was about someone seeing her arrive or leave London Road. A damaged soul, you said."

"The partner must have been watching," said Suzie. "As Vicky got home from work in Andover on Thursday evening, he attacked her as soon as she put her key in the front door. He must have shoved her into the hallway and punched and kicked her until she was unconscious. When Vicky didn't arrive for a group meeting later that evening, a colleague drove round to check on her. The paramedics said it was touch-and-go whether Vicky would make it. She suffered broken ribs, a damaged spleen, and multiple cuts and bruises to her face and stomach. Her fractured skull was a major concern, as there was associated bleeding. Vicky's still in intensive care."

"Did they catch her attacker?" asked Gus.

"He did not know where his wife and children were," said Suzie. "Her colleagues believe Vicky refused to tell him, and that's why the assault was so severe. He phoned his in-laws and threatened them with violence because they told him the charity didn't tell them his family's whereabouts to protect them. The woman's father called the police as soon as the call ended. The police arrested the partner twenty minutes later when he drove to the house, leapt out of the car with a baseball bat, and started hammering on the door. It took four uniformed officers to muscle him to the ground."

"Let's sit in the beer garden for a while before I go inside to get us a drink," said Gus. "This has been a nasty shock."

"It's my fault, Gus," said Suzie. "If I hadn't contacted Vicky to see if there was a way we could work together."

"You can't blame yourself, Suzie. Neil and I met Vicky when we worked on the Gerry Hogan case. I thought she was ready to trust us again, and I knew that if anyone could get her to return to the fold, it was you."

"But I gave the interview to the press," said Suzie. "I stood by the PCC when he gave his spiel. Vicky wasn't there, but it feels like I put a huge target on her back."

"You can't know that, Suzie," said Gus. "Vicky has worked with families in the Andover district for three years. Although she was our connection to the victim support charity because of her background, any work you did together would have benefited both sides."

"I was due to meet her on Wednesday week," said Suzie. "I need to call her colleague in the morning to check on Vicky's progress. I want to visit the hospital if I can. Her friend posted that letter on Saturday. What a mess."

"The partner will face his day in court," said Gus. "As for the wife and kids, they need time to heal. Vicky's colleagues can ensure that happens, and then they'll get re-housed somewhere in the country where the abuser won't find them."

"What about me, Gus?" asked Suzie. "Will he come after me if he can't find them? That man associates me with Vicky Bennison. He blamed Vicky for persuading his wife to leave him and getting her into the refuge. Will I be in danger when he gets out of prison?"

"What do the sentencing guidelines tell us?" asked Gus.

"He could serve as little as three years if the court believes there were mitigating circumstances. I don't believe there were in this instance. The maximum term is sixteen years, but the average sentence is way below that."

"We'll cross that bridge when we come to it, sweetheart," said Gus. "We can speak to Geoff Mercer when the time is right. If there's any hint this guy will attack again, the courts can issue a restraining order."

"He's already shown that won't stop him, Gus."

Gus didn't have the answers Suzie wanted to hear. The system wasn't perfect. Vicky Bennison was the victim of a violent and unprovoked assault. The court's verdict should be cut-and-dried, and it wouldn't surprise him if the partner received the maximum term. How much of that sixteen years would he serve? Ten or twelve, perhaps. If it was ten years, Gus would be seventy-two by then, sat at home in his carpet slippers. What protection could he give? Very little, apart from his security cameras that had gathered cobwebs since he last needed them.

Gus wanted to tell Suzie this guy would be a changed man after ten years in prison. He wanted to say it would be impossible to sustain the level of anger and bitterness shown last week until the day of his release. He wanted to, but he couldn't.

Gus watched Suzie wringing the life out of her handkerchief. She didn't need stress in her condition. Of course, Gus was no expert, but it was reasonable to assume stress could affect the baby's physical and emotional development.

He was about to suggest they give up the idea of a night in the pub and go home when he heard a bicycle bell ring. Brett Penman and Clemency Bentham had arrived. They parked their bikes against the beer garden wall and came down the path to join them.

"You're here already," said Clemency, who still wore her battered bonnet but had changed into a floaty summer dress. Brett strolled behind her in shorts and a t-shirt, looking as if he'd spent two weeks in the Mediterranean.

"Where did you get that suntan, Brett?" asked Gus.

"I can assure you I haven't been lying in the sun," he said. "I've spent several early mornings and afternoons checking on a string of horses out at Beckhampton over the past ten days. If you spent a few hours out of doors, you'd catch the sun too."

"Is everything alright," asked Clemency. She sat next to Suzie straight away.

Gus nodded to Brett that they should leave them to it while they went inside to fetch drinks.

As they stood by the counter waiting for their order, Brett asked what had happened.

"Suzie was hoping to work closely with a woman from a victim support charity on matters associated with domestic abuse. They recently met to sketch out a program Wiltshire Police could help with. But, unfortunately, the partner of one wife the charity was helping attacked Vicky, and now she's in hospital. It's given Suzie a nasty shock."

"They should lock the guy up and throw away the key," said Brett.

"You'll get no argument from me," said Gus.

When they returned outside with their drinks, Suzie and the Reverend were still talking.

"You had better sit, Brett," said Clemency.

Brett did as he was told, and Gus followed suit. He was unsure what was coming next.

"We can't have champagne," said Clemency, "but we can still celebrate the news. Suzie is expecting. Isn't that wonderful news? I get so few christenings to perform. Gus, I do hope you'll do me the honour."

Brett and Clemency raised their glasses and offered a toast.

"You're very kind. We haven't thought that far ahead,

Reverend," said Gus. "You know where I stand on religious matters. We planned to tell everyone the news next week."

"Sorry, Gus," said Suzie. "Clemency thought there was something odd about me suddenly switching to non-alcoholic drinks. Her mind took her in every direction when she saw me in tears when they arrived. It was better to tell her there was nothing seriously wrong with me and that I was eleven weeks pregnant. My emotions are all over the place, and the attack on Vicky tipped me over the edge."

"I put Brett in the picture while we were inside," said Gus.

"I told Suzie not to blame herself, Gus," said Clemency. "The blame lies squarely on the shoulders of the monster who abused his wife and children and then attacked the one person who gave the poor woman the courage to leave him. I'll pray for them tonight. Of course, I should pray for him too, but I must draw the line somewhere."

"Was the pregnancy planned?" asked Brett.

"No way," said Suzie. "It was a happy accident."

"I echo that sentiment," said Gus. "I admit it came as a surprise. But we sat down and discussed matters like sensible adults, and thirty seconds later, we agreed we wanted this baby more than anything."

Gus saw the look Clemency gave Brett Penman. He was undecided what the look meant. The Reverend could have been wondering whether they would ever be in a similar position or checking if she should ask if he and Suzie would get married before the baby arrived.

"Have you two eaten?" asked Brett.

"We thought we'd eat here," said Gus, looking for Suzie's reaction.

"I want nothing more than a lighter bite," said Suzie.

"I'll join you," said Clemency.

When the landlord called last orders, Brett and Clemency disappeared into the gloom at the top of the beer garden to make their way home. Gus went inside to settle the bill but found the veterinary surgeon had beaten him to it.

"Special occasion, was it?" asked the landlord.

"The first Monday in September," said Gus. "a Canadian custom, I expect."

Gus and Suzie left the pub through the front door and walked up the lane to the bungalow.

"I asked Clemency to keep the news under her bonnet until next week," said Suzie.

"If you can't trust her with a secret, we're in trouble," said Gus.

Tuesday, 4 September 2018

GUS HAD SHOWERED and made his way to the kitchen to start breakfast before Suzie made a move. He knew she was still coming to terms with what happened to Vicky Bennison. Between them, Brett and Clemency had persuaded Suzie she shouldn't blame herself, but until they convinced Suzie that Vicky was out of danger, she would remain anxious.

"I'll call the charity as soon as I get to work this morning," she said when she joined him. "I want to check on Vicky's condition with the person who wrote that letter. Then, if I can arrange a visit to see Vicky in the hospital this evening, I'll get a message to you."

"Fair enough," said Gus. "We hope to start interviews today. Most of those will be in Swindon. Just text me when you know the details. We'll eat at home tonight, anyway, so leave dinner to me."

"Thank you, darling," said Suzie.

Breakfast was a quiet affair, but Gus was happy Suzie finished her bowl of cereals and yoghurt.

"Are we ready for the off?" he asked as the kitchen clock ticked around to eight-fifteen.

"I suppose so," said Suzie. "It's cooler this morning, thank goodness."

"I don't need to risk opening my windows on the Focus today, " Gus said. "I'll have to consider another minor problem to present to a garage owner in Swindon."

"Are you thinking of buying a new car?" asked Suzie.

"Heavens, no," said Gus. "Our altered circumstances might encourage me to hunt for a second-hand family saloon next year, but a new car would be extravagant in the extreme."

As they stood beside the Golf and the Focus, Gus could tell from how she looked at his motor two minutes later that Suzie had other ideas on the car situation. The argument was far from resolved. He hoped the Focus couldn't read minds. They had a series of trips to Swindon and back to negotiate together over the coming days.

"See you somewhen this evening," said Suzie.

Gus hardly had time to get comfortable in his driver's seat before the Golf had left the driveway. He followed more conservatively along the lane until traffic on the Lydeway allowed him to close the gap. As he passed the London Road entrance, Suzie waved to him as she reached the steps leading to the main building's front door.

Thirty minutes later, Gus parked beneath the Crime Review Team office and prepared to travel up in the lift.

Lydia's Mini was to his left, and Neil's car on his right. He heard a car arriving as he pressed the lift button.

"Morning, guv,"

It was Blessing Umeh, full of the joys of early September and a new love interest.

"Ready to get stuck into our new case, Blessing?" asked Gus.

"Can't wait, guv," said Blessing. "After dinner last night, I considered what I read yesterday in the murder file. There are so many unanswered questions. The detectives had too many unidentified vehicles and persons of interest. If we were discussing one of your famous jigsaws, they were missing the straight-edged outside pieces."

Gus laughed.

"That's not a bad analogy, Blessing."

Luke Sherman was last to arrive. As he parked on the end of the rank next to Blessing's Nissan Micra, she and Gus held the lift and waited.

"When I was a girl," Blessing continued, "my mother used to collect the straight-edged pieces for the larger puzzles and kept them separate in a small bag in the box. One of those bags the banks used to use for coins. My father accused her of cheating, but I thought it was clever."

"It would help if we could use a similar ploy when tackling complicated cases, Blessing," said Gus.

"Morning, guv," said Luke. "How are you today, Blessing? Did Jamie BT call you as promised?"

"He did," said Blessing as they rode to the first floor. "Jamie's taking me to dinner tomorrow evening. I've warned my mother she will need to call me no later than six o'clock, or she'll miss me."

"That's good to hear," said Luke. "You should strike out on your own, Blessing. At twenty-two, I'd cut the apron strings, and my parents knew better than to try to learn what I was doing twenty-four seven."

Gus kept quiet. His experience of the generation gap with his parents had been troublesome at times. However, listening to Lydia and the others over the past six months had made him realise the issues he'd gone through were nothing as traumatic as younger people had to grapple with today.

The prospect of what challenges his son, or daughter, might pose was something he hoped he and Suzie could handle. So far, their age difference hadn't caused friction. But, if he was still around when his child was twenty-two, the same age as Blessing, would he avoid alienating Suzie and their child with his antiquated opinions of right and wrong?

As Gus followed Luke and Blessing into the office, he decided to park that potential thorny issue until Saturday afternoon at the allotment sat outside his shed.

Neil stood, waiting for Gus to reach his desk.

"I gave Jake Latimer a call last night, guv,"

"Right, let me check what everyone needs to do today," said Gus. "Then you can give me the low-down on how Sengupta and Spencer handled this case. Luke, what's the plan for this morning?"

"Matt Merchant can see us at eleven o'clock, guv," said Luke. "They've got a busy day. But the apprentice isn't at college, so Harry Simpkins can check what she's doing while the boss gets interviewed. Merchant will relieve Harry once we've finished, and that should be it for the garage person-nel, won't it?"

"I don't see any reason to speak to Ms Buckland," said Gus. "Did you tell Matt Merchant who was coming or tell him what to look for?"

"I couldn't give him details, guv," said Luke. "You hadn't indicated who was going."

"The Chief Constable is eager we don't go anywhere alone in the future," said Gus.

"That's my fault," sighed Blessing. "Sorry, guv."

"Not altogether, Blessing," said Gus. "The Chief Constable told me to take Alex or Neil with me for interviews when I returned to work. My consultant role means I can't make an arrest. So, no more flying solo for any of us. Alex and Lydia can visit the garage at eleven. I'll meet you there; you'll understand why later. Did you arrange appointments for this afternoon, Luke?"

"Not specifically, guv. Eve Chaloner will be at home on Shrivenham Road throughout the day. I just need to call her to say when someone's arriving."

"Neil and Blessing can handle that meeting and leave as soon as you've made the call. What about the detectives?"

"Raj Sengupta is in his office every day this week, guv. Tom Spencer won't be easy to reach; he's working north of Lyneham. They've had another rash of thefts of agricultural machinery deep in the countryside. Tom's travelling between farms in Christian Malford and Dauntsey Lock."

"When Alex and Lydia arrive at the garage, I'll drive out to Gablecross," said Gus. "The Chief Constable can't complain if I meet a fellow DI without someone holding my hand. So keep trying to locate Tom Spencer, and perhaps we can meet with him if he finds his way back to civilisation."

"Okay, guv," said Luke. "Before I leave the office, I'll confirm arrangements with the people on Ponting Street. Tom Spencer got statements from; Catherine Fryer, Stan Jones, and Ralph Robinson."

"Who the heck is Ralph Robinson?" asked Gus.

"He was the witness who saw the white-van man arguing with Richard Chaloner, guv," said Luke.

"Did his name appear in the murder file?" said Neil. "I didn't spot it."

"It was in one appendix, hidden away," said Luke. "He wasn't supposed to be on Ponting Street that morning."

"How old is he?" asked Gus.

"He was sixty-eight at the time of the murder, guv," said Luke. "His wife thought he'd driven out to South Marston to tend to his parent's grave."

"Did he get lost?" asked Neil. "Robinson was sixty-eight. It happens."

"Careful, Neil," said Gus. "You're entering dangerous territory."

"Sorry, guv," said Neil. "Did he admit to Tom Spencer what attracted him to Ponting Street?"

"It's only a short walk from Manchester Road, guv," suggested Alex.

"I'll call Eve Chaloner now, Neil," said Luke.

"Thanks, Luke. It will stop me from digging a bigger hole."

Even though he worked in Salisbury, Gus was well aware the streets around Manchester Road became known as an area where sex workers worked in reasonably large numbers in years gone by. Residents had worked hard, with much success, to rid their neighbourhood of that reputation. Two years ago, and only weeks before the murder they were now investigating took place, the coverage of a trial of a double murderer led to its resurfacing. That killer had a history of soliciting for prostitution around Manchester Road, and it was there that he came to know one of his victims. According to comments in the media, prostitution was rife in the town, an accusation many local people believed unfair.

"Was Robinson visiting a lady friend on Ponting Street, or was he driving past the garage on his way to Manchester Road?" asked Gus.

"Wiltshire Police closed several establishments on either side of the Chaloner murder in 2016, guv," said Neil. "I remember places on Commercial Road, Brunel Crescent, and York Road getting their name in the local press."

"The work undertaken by the authorities and the charities involved drove the problem off the streets and behind closed doors," said Gus. "We touched on this aspect during the Laura Mallinder enquiry. I recall the phrase 'pop-ups' getting used for places that might exist for only a day or two. Girls from Poland and Romania, trafficked here by criminal gangs, got moved on as soon as their handlers found alternate premises. A moving target is always more difficult to hit."

Lydia tutted.

"I meant the buildings from which the girls operated, not the girls themselves," said Gus.

"I know, guv," said Lydia. "I was bemoaning the fact this business always seems to put vulnerable women's lives at risk."

"Wiltshire Police said there was a distinct possibility the man convicted of murdering those two young women could be responsible for other unsolved murders," said Alex. "There was an eight-year gap between the killings."

"They had no forensic evidence connecting him to any open cases, Alex," said Neil. "However, that's not to say he hadn't committed other offences."

"I'm certain there would be others," said Gus. "I don't

think he'd have gone eight years without hunting out another victim."

"We can't link that to the Chaloner case, though, guv," said Neil.

"I think that's a given, Neil," said Gus. "We'll ask Ralph Robinson what he was doing that morning. Then, if needs be, we'll interview him at home in front of his wife."

"That makes a change, guv," said Blessing. "You usually threaten them with getting dragged into a police station for an interview under caution."

"Horses for courses," said Gus. "We need more detail on that white van and its driver."

"Alex and I won't need to leave for Ponting Street for an hour, guv," said Lydia. "What can we do in the meantime?"

"When are you leaving here, guv?" asked Neil. "Can we give you a lift?"

"No, Neil. I need my car," said Gus. "Anyway, I need you to tell me quickly what you heard from Jake Latimer."

"You might not like what you're going to hear, guv."

Chapter Five

"THIS CASE WAS the final straw for DI Sengupta's ongoing involvement as a Senior Investigating Officer, guv," said Neil. "Raj attended the murder scene with Tom Spencer and arranged the house-to-house enquiries starting the same afternoon. Unfortunately, the occupants of many of the properties on either side of the road were at work. Uniformed officers returned the following day to revisit those addresses hoping to find someone at home."

"Did Sengupta not think to make the visits the same evening?" asked Gus.

"It appears not, guv," said Neil. "Tom Spencer thought the morning run was a waste of resources. So instead, he wanted to carry out house-to-house visits in the streets on either side."

"Raj's plan might not have been as daft as Jake imagined, Neil," said Gus. "Catherine Fryer worked a morning shift and was home in the afternoons. So what's to say someone didn't see the white van man at eleven o'clock? They could have heard everything the guy and Chaloner said. They may have told the police what they were arguing over."

"Then they went to work in the afternoon," said Neil. "I suppose that makes sense."

"Did the morning run turn up any new leads?" asked Gus.

"No, guv," said Neil. "Raj Sengupta sent Tom Spencer to the autopsy on Wednesday morning. Tom got Stuart Fitzwalter's thoughts on time and cause of death and returned to Gablecross. Raj had gone home with a migraine. Tom debriefed the morning run with the uniforms and then rang Sengupta at home. Raj insisted it was a robbery, plain and simple. He told Tom they needed to find the twenty-two-carat gold chain. It was pointless worrying about the cash because it was untraceable. Tom pointed out that if someone offered the chain to a guy in the pub and fifty quid changed hands, the odds of catching the killer that way were miniscule. Raj told Tom to alert local jewellers and pawnbrokers."

"If our killer was as meticulous as I believe," said Gus, "then he wouldn't do anything as rash as offloading an expensive gold chain within days of the murder. But, did the gold chain ever surface?"

"No, guv," said Neil.

"Did they send forensics to the ATM where the killer used the bank card?" asked Gus.

"Stuart Fitzwalter arrived at the garage before Sengupta and Spencer. The police surgeon believed the attacker wore gloves. Raj thought that meant the ATM was a waste of time. Even if the killer removed a glove to key in the PIN....."

"Exactly. Hundreds of people could have used the ATM in the town centre before forensics checked for prints. To cover his backside, Raj should have checked, regardless. They could hang onto the prints and partials to try for a match against a suspect. If they ever identified one. Then they could destroy the rest.

"It wasn't the best start to an investigation, was it, guv?" said Neil.

"I sense there's more, Neil," said Gus. "It can wait until we get back from Swindon. I'll have heard Raj Sengupta's version of events by then too. Blessing, when you speak to Eve Chaloner, can you get an accurate description of that gold chain, please?"

"Got it, guv," said Blessing. "Anything else?"

Gus shook his head. Luke gave Neil the nod that he had informed Eve Chaloner they would be with her within the hour. Neil and Blessing made their way to the lift.

"I wonder why Gus told you to ask Eve Chaloner about the gold chain," said Neil.

"She will use words that mean nothing to you, Neil," said Blessing. "You men only see a chunky piece of bling. With rings, bracelets, and necklaces, we girls see something else."

"I don't get it," said Neil. "What's that?"

"Commitment," said Blessing.

Meanwhile, back at his desk, Gus wondered what to ask Raj Sengupta—investigating a serious crime such as murder attracted a significant press interest, especially in the first days of an enquiry. The SIO has to resolve tensions surrounding what to disclose and what to hold back concerning the offence. What were the potential consequences in this case of releasing details of the theft of the gold chain?

Gus recognised Raj was probably an expert in media strategy, something he'd failed to relate to when he was a serving officer. Ideally, what the police wanted from a press release was to gain information. However, once you invited the media to the party, you often lost control over how they portrayed the information you drip-fed them. So, Raj would have had to manage the balancing act of press interest and minimising misinformation. The press reports on prostitution being a case in point.

Gus had lost count of the times he listened to Geoff Mercer reminding the public that murder was rare. There wasn't a gunman on every street corner in the county. So the media strategy Raj adopted would have aimed to minimise community concern over the fear of crime.

Gus decided he'd waited long enough.

"I'll see you two at eleven," he said to Alex and Lydia.

Luke Sherman wondered when he might make a telling contribution to this enquiry. So far, he'd compiled a list of interviewees and arranged appointments.

"Are you sure you don't want me to come with you, guv?" he asked.

"Not this time, Luke," said Gus. "It would give the game away."

As Gus headed for the lift, he paused.

"If we can't arrange any more interviews, for the time being, Luke, why don't you look at the case from a different angle? Ignore the robbery aspect and dismiss the links to a criminal gang. What other options are there? Who would want to shoot Richard Chaloner, and why? Maybe, the original detective team and ourselves are looking in the wrong place. As I said yesterday, the killer was a local man or woman. Could the killing have been personal? If so, what event in Chaloner's life has everyone missed?"

"Will do, guv," said Luke. At last, he had a meaningful task.

Gus exited the lift and reversed the Ford Focus out of the parking bay. A steady drive to Ponting Street, Swindon, from here, should take him around an hour. Lydia had driven her Mini to work this morning. So she and Alex could leave the office by a quarter past ten and still reach Merchant Motor Repairs by eleven o'clock with her driving.

Traffic on the road to Chippenham was light, and although it increased as he approached the M4 junction beyond Kingston St Michael, Gus felt confident he'd have enough time at the garage to suit his purpose. His timing was spot on. After a clear run on the motorway to blow the cobwebs from his faithful companion's engine, he drew up on the garage forecourt at twenty minutes to the hour. A dark-haired teenager in dark blue overalls looked up from the car she was working on and called to someone at the back of the workshop.

"Matt, we've got a customer."

Matt Merchant emerged from behind the Toyota and Vauxhall cars Anne Marie Buckland and Harry Simpkins were working on. Matt and his two employees were resplendent in matching navy blue outfits. Gus spotted the MMR logo in white lettering on the breast pocket. Not a marketing guru's first choice, but what else could they have used?

"How can I help you, sir?" asked Matt.

Gus studied the thirty-one-year-old man in front of him. Things could go either way; Gus hoped the lad was as genuine as he appeared at first glance.

"I've had this car since it was new," said Gus. "It pains me to admit it, but it's knackered. The dial shows well over a hundred thousand miles on the clock. I'm retired and can't afford to replace it unless I get a reasonable price in part exchange. What can you do to help?"

"We can get you booked in for a full service. As the

saying goes, making a silk purse out of a sow's ear is impossible, but it might add a couple hundred pounds to its value. How does the middle of next week suit you?"

"Someone recommended this place to me," said Gus. "He brought his car here for several years. I can't remember the name of the chap who owned the business then. My neighbour mentioned his name, but it slipped my memory."

"That would have been Mr Chaloner," said Matt. "I've worked here for fifteen years. Richard took me on straight from school. I may have worked on your neighbour's car. What did he drive?"

"Oh, he changed his car every few years," said Gus. "The thing is, he'd heard your Mr Chaloner helped people out in my position. If this Ford Focus showed sixty thousand miles on the clock when I took it to a dealer, I'd have a better chance of trading it in and affording the car I want. If you get my drift."

"I do, and I don't like what I'm hearing," said Matt. "We don't do that here, and Richard Chaloner wouldn't have entertained such an idea either. He was as honest as the day is long, and I intend to follow his lead. Whoever your neighbour is, he's mistaken. What was the customer's name, anyway?"

"He's a near neighbour," said Gus. "You know how it is these days. People speak in passing, but you don't know them well. His first name was Bob or Rod, but the surname, well, now you're asking."

Harry Simpkins had edged away from the Vauxhall and was listening to the conversation.

"You've got visitors in a couple of minutes, Matt," he said.

"Who are you?" Matt Merchant asked Gus. "There's something not right about this. If you spoke to someone who used to bring his car here for servicing, they would have mentioned that Richard died."

"The police thought Richard Chaloner was working with a criminal gang," said Gus. "Either telling them which cars you handled had catalytic converters fitted or receiving the items the gang had stolen."

"That story never appeared in the papers," said Matt. "It was rubbish. Richard wouldn't get involved in any dodgy business. So I reckon you should hang on until my visitors get here. They will want a word."

Gus heard a throaty roar at the end of the street. Lydia had exceeded the speed limit on the motorway. She never listened.

"A red Mini will pull onto the forecourt in a few seconds, Mr Merchant," said Gus, without turning round. "My colleagues are here to interview you and Mr Simpkins."

Lydia stopped beside Gus's Ford Focus, and she and Alex got out.

"Everything okay, guv?" asked Alex.

"Yes, DS Hardy. My work here is done. This business has a clean bill of health. We can discount links to organised crime, past or present. You can continue with questions that will add to our understanding of the events surrounding the day of the murder. I'm off to Gablecross Police Station now to meet with DI Sengupta. Apologies for the deception, Mr Merchant. It was the quickest way to streamline our lines of enquiry."

"I still don't know who you are," said Matt. "I thought the police were supposed to identify themselves."

"I'm a retired Detective Inspector," said Gus. "I returned to work with Wiltshire Police as a consultant. My name's Freeman."

"Well, Mr Freeman," said Matt. "I wish you luck

trading in that Focus if that is your true intention. But, unfortunately, you're right; it's past its sell-by date."

Gus knew it was Lydia stifling a laugh behind his back.

"I'll leave you two to get on with things," he said, getting into the driver's seat.

Alex Hardy and Lydia Logan Barre disappeared inside the garage with Matt Merchant and were soon out of sight behind the Toyota and the Vauxhall. Harry and Anne Marie had resumed work. Their excitement was over for the morning.

ONE MILE AWAY, Neil Davis and Blessing Umeh were in a well-appointed detached house on Shrivenham Road. Eve Chaloner had greeted them at the front door and ushered them into the lounge. Neil was pleased to see coffee came with a choice of biscuits. Blessing would have loved to take one when offered, but she decided her weight suffered enough with the generous helpings of food Jackie Ferris provided.

Neil could understand what attracted Richard Chaloner to Eve. She wore her forty-three years well. The wedding photograph on the sideboard showed Eve's appearance had changed little in the past two years. A few extra grey hairs at the temple, but that was it.

Neil selected a second biscuit, and as they had already introduced themselves, he began the interview in earnest.

"How did you and Richard meet?" he asked.

"I was enjoying a night out in Swindon with work-mates," she replied. "I can't recall whether it was some-one's birthday or a leaving-do. We had plenty of social occasions when I worked at Nationwide. We'd been in one of the town centre pubs for an hour when Richard came in with a friend. I wasn't looking for a relationship at the time."

"Was this soon after you moved to Swindon?" asked Neil.

"A few months," said Eve. "I had been married to John for fourteen years, and when the marriage ended, I needed to leave Warminster. So I found the Swindon job quickly and bought a place in Haydon Wick."

"That was John Allsopp, wasn't it?" asked Neil.

"Yes, we met at work in Westbury, married in 2000, and bought a bigger house in Warminster in 2008. We continued to work together with the same firm. I thought we were happy. However, John changed jobs eighteen months after we moved house. We didn't see one another as often as we had after that, but I didn't suspect he was having an affair."

"The curse of the office Christmas party," said Neil. "When did you realise something was wrong?"

"Soon after that Christmas party at the end of 2013," said Eve. "Her name was Kirsty, and she was only nineteen, for heaven's sake. I didn't ask for the names of the others with whom he had flings."

"Kirsty wasn't the only occasion John strayed then?" said Neil. That was new.

"The wife is always the last to know, isn't she?" said Eve. "I heard from friends at our old firm that John was prolific, and the girls got younger every time. I couldn't accept it. So I filed for divorce in the New Year."

"There had to be a good reason for you to get together with Richard after that experience," said Blessing.

"Richard was a gentleman," said Eve. "I couldn't believe he hadn't been married before. He told me he'd been waiting for the right girl. I asked my friends at work if they had heard any stories. I suspected I would find a string of broken hearts in the town or that he was broke thanks to child maintenance payments. They could tell me nothing detrimental. There had been girlfriends, but no one serious. Richard had many friends and belonged to several clubs and societies. The Folk Club in Highworth, CAMRA–the Campaign for Real Ale, and the Round Table. Of course, he loved his cars and cycling."

"You didn't wait long to get married, despite the problems that ended your first marriage," said Neil.

"Why should we wait?" said Eve. "We were meant to be together, DS Davis. I truly believe that I found my soulmate."

Blessing knew what Eve meant. Who could have predicted such a tragic turn of events only six months after the happy day in that wedding photograph?

"After you left Warminster, did you have occasion to speak to your former husband?"

"I haven't spoken to John since the day I left and returned home to my parents," said Eve.

"How would John have reacted to news that you had married again?" asked Neil.

"None of his damn business," said Eve.

"You must have enquired what he did after you left him," said Neil. "Surely one of your friends would have mentioned if he got married, lost his job, or broke a leg skiing. I find it hard to believe you knew nothing of what happened after spending fourteen years together. We know John knew you moved to Swindon and got a job with Nationwide."

"I don't think he and Kirsty lasted long," said Eve. "Other than that, I don't have any contact with my old Westbury work colleagues. I visit my parents in Westbury occasionally, but they never mention John, and I don't ask for news."

"Did you ever visit Richard at the garage?" asked Blessing.

"When we first started seeing one another, I admit I drove past the garage to take a look. I was still working at Nationwide and popped around during my lunch break. I admired Richard running his own business, even though it was a small affair."

"Did you meet Matt Merchant and Harry Simpkins?" asked Blessing.

"Matt, Jess and the children came to our wedding. Harry and Thelma were there too. I had met none of them before that day. Over the next six months, we spoke on the phone if I rang the garage to speak to Richard, and he was with a customer. Richard didn't mix with them socially. Does that sound snobbish?"

"Not at all," said Neil. "We understand you heard the news of Richard's death while on holiday in Northern Greece," said Neil. "Was that with colleagues from Nationwide?"

"One of my best friends was getting married at the end of the month. We had flown from Bristol International on Sunday. The hotel manager took me into his office late on Tuesday afternoon to break the terrible news. It was devastating. I flew home the next morning and went home to my parents. I cried for days. Richard didn't have an enemy in the world. If someone pointed a gun at him and asked for money, he would have handed over everything he had. They didn't need to shoot him."

"Did you buy Richard the gold chain?" asked Blessing.

"It was a wedding present," said Eve.

"I bet it looked good on him. Do you have any photos?"

"On my phone," said Eve. She found the photo in seconds. Blessing imagined Eve often looked at that photo and thought of what might have been.

"It was a Miami Cuban Link chain," said Eve. "Twenty inches long, four millimetres wide, in twenty-two-carat gold with a box lock clasp."

"Could I have a copy of that photo, please?" asked Blessing. "The chain never surfaced during the original investigation. It might be a long shot, but at least we can better describe what we're searching for."

Eve agreed to send the image to Blessing's phone. Neil tried to think of questions they should ask, but the answers they had got so far didn't prompt many plausible follow-up questions.

"I hope you make more progress with the case this time, " Eve sighed. "Despite the hours the detectives from Gable-cross put in, especially Tom Spencer, they didn't find a clue where to look for Richard's killer."

"Our boss asks us to pose different questions of the people who got interviewed the first time around," said Blessing. "That way, we get different answers."

"We still need to know the right questions to ask," said Neil. He stood up to leave.

"Thank you for your time this morning, Mrs Chaloner. We'll get in touch if there's anything else we need to ask."

"Did you return to work at Nationwide after Richard's murder?" asked Blessing.

"No, dear," said Eve. "We disposed of our individual properties when we married, bought this house with the proceeds, and still had a little to put by for our pension pot. The plan was for me to take a year out and then find a part-time job. When Richard died, I learned he had taken out an insurance policy when he opened the business, which meant

I could stay a woman of leisure as long as I wished. I'm itching for something to occupy my days now, so maybe I'll hunt for that part-time job in a month or two. There's no rush."

"Was there any particular reason for the gap year?" asked Neil.

"We were trying for a baby," replied Eve.

"I'm sorry," said Neil.

"It was foolish, but although doctors consider me ancient, we both thought it was a gamble that might pay off. No need to apologise; you have a job to do."

Blessing followed Neil to the front door. She glanced at another wedding photo as she walked past the Welsh dresser.

"Who was the mate with Richard that first night you met in the pub?"

"Jeff Hughes," said Eve. "He was Richard's best man at the wedding. They went to school together and joined several clubs and societies together, too. Jeff's got a window-cleaning business. You don't see him up a ladder at a residential property like mine. Jeff and his crew are usually dangling off the side of an enormous building in a cradle. You wouldn't catch me anywhere near one of those."

"We'll let you get on with your day," said Blessing. "Bye for now."

Once they were back in Neil's car, he pulled away from the kerb and started the journey back to the Old Police Station office.

"You got an excellent description of the necklace," said Neil. "What was behind the random question as we were leaving?"

"Gus enjoys a Lieutenant Columbo moment," said Blessing. "I wondered why Eve was home in the daytime.

Of course, the insurance money could give her motive to kill her husband, but I believe her when she says she only learned of the policy after the murder."

"I agree," said Neil. "We hadn't heard of this Jeff Hughes, Chaloner's best man, before, had we?"

"Hughes was a man Chaloner knew well," said Blessing. "They were the same age, and he was someone with his own business. Who do we know, thirty-five to forty-five years old, driving a white van? Might a window cleaner wear white overalls?"

"It's a thought, but if Hughes were best man at Richard's wedding, Merchant and Simpkins would have met him. Unless they lied to Tom Spencer, he couldn't be the white van man arguing with Richard Chaloner."

"You're right, of course, Neil," said Blessing. "Silly me. I jumped in too quickly again."

"Not necessarily; think what it said about Chaloner in the murder file. Something which Eve Chaloner confirmed just now. Chaloner was gregarious, popular, and had a wide circle of friends. It's possible the man on the forecourt knew Chaloner through the Folk Club, the CAMRA crowd, or Round Table."

"What is Round Table, Neil?" asked Blessing. "Do they do re-enactments of Arthurian legend?

"It's a non-political and non-religious organisation for young men aged between eighteen and forty-five," said Neil. "Members believe in achieving change and excellence in themselves and their local communities. There are branches worldwide whose motto is to adopt, adapt, and improve. Round Table attracts professionals, such as Chaloner and Hughes. Some think it helps them get on in life."

"Did you ever get asked to join, Neil?" asked Blessing.

"No, and I wouldn't join the Freemasons, either. I want

to get as far as possible on merit, not by being part of a secret society."

"We should double-check the murder file," said Blessing. "Did DS Spencer interview people from these organisations where Chaloner was an active member?"

"That will be our first job after we get back, Blessing," said Neil. "You might have found the right place to look for the white van man. Well done."

Chapter Six

IN PONTING STREET, Matt Merchant closed his office door and sat opposite the two detectives.

"Perhaps we can start again, Mr Merchant," said Alex. "I'm DS Hardy, and my colleague is Ms Logan Barre. We work with the Crime Review Team from Wiltshire Police, and we're taking a fresh look into Richard Chaloner's murder."

"I'll help in any way I can," said Matt.

"You said when we were outside that you started here straight from school," said Alex.

"My father suggested I should ask Richard for a job. He'd met him at a Round Table branch meeting. Richard had Harry here working with him, and the business was growing. They needed an extra pair of hands. I liked cars. Harry's a decent sort, and Richard made the garage an enjoyable place to come to work every day. Richard aimed to offer a quality service with a smile. He reckoned you were more likely to get customers to stay with you, year in and year out, that way. Richard pointed out several other lock-up outfits similar to ours that charged over the odds for shoddy work and treated their customers like dirt that went to the wall. We're still standing."

"The detectives in the original investigation asked whether anything unusual occurred in the days leading up to the murder," said Alex. "Has an incident come to mind that you might have forgotten at the time?"

"That chap Spencer asked what we did that Monday," said Matt. "Then they checked we were where we said later that evening. Other than that, they didn't dig deeper into the months or weeks before Richard died."

"Are you telling us you had instances in the previous months where you, or Harry, suspected something?" asked Alex. "Did strangers arrive at the garage looking for Richard, or talk to him outside, so you couldn't hear what they said?"

"No, nothing like that. Most of our business came from existing customers. Richard didn't encourage cold-callers, but we had the occasional visit from a rep trying to sell us the latest gadget for identifying faults, especially in the newer models."

"Did his new wife pop in for a chat or any of his friends?" asked Lydia.

"Eve didn't visit the garage," said Matt. "She rang him from time to time before they got married and after. They made a fine couple. Richard's death was a tragedy."

"Richard was single for so many years while you worked here," said Lydia. "Did it surprise you when he announced he was marrying Eve?"

"He always did something in the evenings and at weekends," said Matt. "Richard wasn't short of friends. I always thought he'd settle down eventually. The way he behaved with people here, day-in and day-out, was how he was in his social life. There was only one side to Richard, the sunny side."

"Let's switch our attention to the seventh of November," said Alex. "When was the last time you saw Richard Chaloner alive?"

"Ten to six that Monday night," said Matt. "I walked outside through the side door and ran to my car. It was still raining. As I passed Richard's bicycle, I spotted he had a flat tyre. I went back to the door and shouted for him. He was sitting here, in this chair, catching up with paperwork. He came outside and realised someone had deliberately slashed the tyre."

"Neither of you had seen or heard anyone outside during the day?" asked Alex.

"It must have happened in the afternoon," said Matt. "We had the front doors open until the wind got up and the rainstorm began. One of us would have spotted someone walking up the side of the garage."

"Who might want to slash Richard's tyres; any ideas?"

"Not a clue," said Matt. "It could have been kids. However, most of them were at school. This street is home to mostly elderly people anyway, and we don't suffer too much teenage vandalism on Ponting Street."

"You offered Richard a lift home to Shrivenham Road, didn't you?" asked Lydia. "That was out of your way."

"Yeah, I drove to Wootton Bassett to play football on Monday nights. I made the offer, but I knew he would do it his way. Richard had his wet-weather gear hung up behind me, a repair kit in the drawer of the filing cabinet—everything he needed to keep that old bike of his on the road. A drop of rain wouldn't stop Richard from cycling to and from work. So, I left him to it and drove to meet with my mates."

"Did you see anyone near the garage as you left?" asked Alex.

"The rain kept people indoors until later that night. I think the storm had passed by eight or half-past. Everything was quieter when I drove home after football."

"You were first to arrive in the morning. Was that normal?" asked Alex.

"I didn't think I was the first," said Matt, "because Richard's bike was there."

"Didn't you spot he hadn't repaired the tyre?" asked Lydia.

"No, I was probably looking at the sports pages. I had picked up a paper from the newsagents at the bottom of the road where I live. I tried the door, found it locked, and so I opened the door and walked in."

"We know both you and Harry had keys. Didn't it strike you as odd to find the door locked, even though you thought Richard was inside?"

"Check for yourself. It's a Yale lock, and unless we prop it open during the day when we have the front doors shut, it closes automatically."

"You only got as far as the doorway, is that right?" asked Alex.

"I heard Harry whistling as he walked up the pathway. I stepped inside and looked across to this office, but nobody was here, although the lights were on. Harry joined me inside, switched on the workshop lights, and we saw Richard straightaway. Harry made a move towards him, but I stopped him. There was nothing anyone could do. I could see the chest wound from where I stood. I went outside and called the police on my mobile, and Harry joined me outside to wait for them. We didn't touch a thing, apart from Harry turning on the lights."

"Who told you there had been a robbery?" asked Alex.

"Harry had spotted Richard's wallet on the floor near the office door as we were leaving to call the police. He pointed it out to one of the uniformed officers when they got here. The officer placed a marker beside it but didn't touch it. Detective Sergeant Spencer arrived a few minutes later and started getting things organised. It was a shambles before that. Ten minutes later, another van arrived with the CSI crew. It was Piccadilly Circus in here for several hours. Finally, they asked Harry and me to step outside while they collected evidence."

"Did you have any idea how much cash Richard carried with him?" asked Lydia.

"Richard wouldn't have discussed that with Harry or me."

"Did Richard wear any jewellery?" asked Alex.

"Not before he got married. After that, he wore a wedding ring and that flashy gold chain. It wasn't as chunky as the ones the rappers wear. It was more elegant than that. Richard liked it. That was the key thing."

"Did Eve give Richard the chain?" asked Lydia.

"A wedding present, I believe," said Matt.

"You didn't approve," said Alex.

"When you're working with machinery, you don't want things swinging loosely around your neck," said Matt. "Richard pulled the zip up to the top of his overalls, which reduced the risk of an accident."

"I notice your navy blue overalls have a collar," said Alex. "Are you still using the same brand?"

"The same brand and colour," said Matt, "we just changed the logo."

"So with the collar and the zip pulled up to the neck, it

might not have been obvious Richard was wearing a gold chain?"

"It wouldn't be easy to see, no."

"Unless it was someone who knew him and knew he had worn the chain every day for the past six months."

"I suppose so," said Matt. "But if it was a robbery, the killer might have hunted for items to steal."

"This office was largely undisturbed," said Alex. "They didn't drag drawers out of the desk or the filing cabinets. Richard's wet-weather gear and jacket were still hanging on pegs on the wall behind you. They were selective, weren't they? After all, the only item they lifted from this office was the bank card."

"If Richard was doing paperwork when they got here, he would have had the bank card on the desk. I told the police that."

"You did, so did Harry. Both of you told the police the PIN was on a scrap of paper pinned to the noticeboard. Not a great idea, was it?"

"I told Richard it was asking for trouble," said Matt. "He said he trusted Harry and me. He asked when the last time was that someone was in this office without one of us. I couldn't even remember it happening. So there you are then, he said, it's not a problem."

"When did DS Spencer return to ask about the three men seen outside the garage on Monday?" asked Alex.

"Later in the week," said Matt. "The garage was off-limits until the CSI crew had finished their work. I called the bank to stop the card. That's when they told me the card got used the night before, and the killer had taken another four hundred quid. There wasn't enough left in the account to pay our wages that week. Eve flew home on Wednesday from her hen week. I wanted to ask her what she wanted us to do with the business, but I knew she must be grieving. I called the car owners we had booked in and told them we needed to re-schedule. We closed the place until the following Monday, the fourteenth. DS Spencer visited me at home in Elmina Road and asked about somebody Richard's age trying to get his van fixed mid-morning. I'd been working on a BMW that morning and took little notice. I couldn't help him."

"Did you see the man with the van?" asked Lydia. "How did you know he was Richard's age?"

"Spencer said an eyewitness told them the man was between thirty-five and forty-five years old," said Matt. "I could only offer a general description of the man and his van. I had the engine running while I was tuning the BMW, plus the radio was playing on the workbench at the side. So I only heard the odd word of their conversation."

"Had you seen him before?" asked Lydia.

"He wasn't one of our regulars," said Matt.

"Did you think he and Richard knew one another? Could they have been friends?"

Matt Merchant thought for a moment.

"When DS Spencer asked me at the time, I said I didn't know. Harry saw and heard more than I did. I thought anything I said only tallied with what Harry told him, so I didn't bother. Spencer didn't need to hear the same thing twice."

"Two years on, you think there was something you should have commented on, is that it?" asked Alex.

"I don't know that it would have made much difference to the investigation, but when I thought about it weeks later, I reckon Richard *did* know the guy. Where from, I don't know. He wasn't at the wedding, so he wasn't a close friend. He thought he could use their connection to persuade

Richard to fit him in, regardless of how busy we were. Harry told me Richard stuck to his guns, told the bloke his regular customers came first, and he drove off with a flea in his ear."

"An acquaintance then, from one club or organisation he frequented," said Alex.

"That fits with the image I saw," said Matt. "That's what I reasoned it must have been when I sat and remembered the incident."

"Richard didn't tell you what the argument was over?" asked Lydia.

"Not a word," said Matt. "We were busy."

"DS Spencer asked whether either of you saw a young white lad in his early twenties hanging around on the other side of the road," said Alex. "Are you sure you didn't see anyone?

"The front doors were still open between one and two," said Lydia. "You said you would have spotted anyone creeping up the side of the garage to slash Richard's bicycle tyre."

"Ponting Street is close to the railway station," said Matt. "Only a five-minute walk away. It could have been a total stranger looking for a vulnerable target. I don't have to spell it out for you."

Alex and Lydia knew the Swindon railway station had become a gateway for young people bringing class A drugs into the West Country from London. The excellent public transport links to the capital meant criminals sent youngsters to ferry drugs via the town.

"No, Mr Merchant, we understand the situation," said Lydia. "We aim to find and safeguard vulnerable children used to transport drugs and cash. However, it's important to recognise these youngsters are victims. We know what harm these networks cause within our communities and strive to ensure any gangs that commit offences in Wiltshire get identified, arrested, and punished. It's possible the youngster Mrs Fryer saw was a day visitor from London. We'll follow up on that line of enquiry. If that was the case, it's no surprise DS Spencer's team couldn't trace him."

"What did you make of the last person of interest identified by the detective team?" asked Alex,

"Was that the West-Indian guy and his girlfriend?" asked Matt. "We had closed the doors by then. The old guy, Stan, told the police he saw a bloke looking in the window. If he was, it couldn't have been for long."

"Why do you say that?" asked Lydia.

"According to DS Spencer, the man was short, stocky, and muscular. He was built like a rugby front-row forward. Have you seen those doors? The windows at the top must be six feet off the ground. I couldn't stand on tiptoe for too long, and I'm fairly fit. That guy or the girl Spencer mentioned could have slashed the bicycle tyre. After half-past two, when we shut the doors, it would have been easier for someone to slip up the side of the garage, use a knife, and slip away again. I saw no one at the window, nor did I hear the car they drove away in Stan reported to the police."

"Had you seen anyone matching their description near the garage?" asked Alex.

Matt Merchant shook his head.

"Don't misunderstand me. We don't discriminate in any fashion when it comes to working on people's cars. The only thing Richard insisted on was that people paid the bill when it was due. I work the same way. If that chap was a regular customer, he needn't have tried peeking through the window. He'd know that if he gave a quick tap on the side door, we'd answer."

"You know Stan Jones from over the road, then?" asked Lydia. "Does he bring his car here?"

"Old Stan hasn't been well enough to drive for a few years now, and he's confined to that house. He's got his telly, but when he can't find anything to watch, he sits and looks out of the window. He doesn't miss much."

"Is his wife still with him?" asked Lydia.

"No, she died several years ago now. Cancer."

"It can't be much fun living alone when your health is failing," said Alex.

"Young Stan drops in to visit his father," said Matt. "He's a long-distance lorry driver whose trips take him across the UK and Europe. I don't know where he lives when he's not sleeping in his cab, and old Stan hasn't mentioned a daughter-in-law or grandchildren."

"How old is the son?" asked Lydia.

"Mid-thirties now, I imagine," said Matt.

"I think that's enough for this morning," said Alex. "We may need to get back to you in the next few days. We'd like to speak to Harry now if that's okay?"

"Sure, I'll see how far Anne Marie has got with that Toyota and send Harry to you."

When Matt Merchant had left the room, Lydia puffed out her cheeks.

"Gus was right. If you ask people to recount an experience, they *always* add something they forgot the first time. Matt thought about the white van man six weeks after the murder and realised something about how he and Chaloner spoke suggested they did have a connection. That's something we can chase."

"Matt also associated the young stranger with the drug

trade because he's lived and worked near the station for years. That's a typical reaction. Every teenage kid isn't a criminal, but public perception is that if they're hanging around on a street corner, they must be up to no good. The murder file mentioned the young Matt Merchant got into a few scrapes which could have led him down a different path."

"If he saw a young man behaving like the one Mrs Fryer saw, Matt would have known whether they were guilty or innocent."

"Matt's views on the third person of interest are in line with ours," said Alex. "The coloured man or his girlfriend were most likely candidates for slashing the bicycle tyre."

"Why, though?" asked Lydia. "That's the thing we can't pin down. What did they have against Richard Chaloner? Perhaps Harry Simpkins will shed light on matters."

The office door opened, and Harry paused before entering. Alex nodded for him to sit in the boss's chair. He could tell it made Harry uncomfortable. Good; it might cause him to slip up.

"Good morning, Harry. I'm DS Hardy with Wiltshire Police. My colleague, Ms Logan Barre and I work with a Crime Review Team. Our task is to find Richard's killer. You were already working here with Richard when Matt started, is that correct?"

"I knew Richard's father," said Harry. "When Richard started the business, Richard asked if I'd come to work for him. He needed someone with experience. I've worked in the trade since I left school at fifteen in 1970."

"When was the last time you saw Richard alive?" asked Lydia.

"When I left work at half-past five on Monday evening."

"Did you notice anything unusual in the alleyway as you left?" asked Alex. "Was there anyone loitering near the garage?"

"I didn't spot the puncture if that's what you mean. It was raining cats and dogs, and I just wanted to get home. I kept my head down and walked as quickly as these old legs would carry me. I didn't see a single vehicle or person walking until I got to the end of Alfred Street. Mrs Fellows was hurrying back home with her dog. She lives three doors further on to us."

"It must have shocked you when you reached work that morning?" asked Lydia.

"Matt was in the doorway. I wasn't far from getting here first when he turned into Ponting Street. With his younger legs, Matt had opened up by the time I arrived."

"So, Matt waited before entering. Is that what you're saying?" asked Alex.

"Only a second or two. When I asked later in the day why he paused, Matt said he couldn't make out why the office lights were on, but Richard wasn't there. I turned on the lights in the workshop and then wished I hadn't."

"Why did you turn on the lights?" asked Lydia.

"It's what we always did. Whoever got here first opened up, switched on the lights, and got the kit ready for each car we were due to work on. We were a team. We've got different players now, but we're still a team. Everyone helps everyone else."

"Matt told us you wanted to go to Richard, but he stopped you," said Alex.

"I didn't think," said Harry. "At first, I thought he'd fainted. I'm the first-aider, so it was natural to see what I could do to help. Matt told me if the office lights were still on, it meant Richard had been here all night. Even from where we stood, I could tell he was right. Richard had been dead for hours. We went outside touching nothing, and Matt called the police. As we passed Richard's bike, Matt pointed and said Richard didn't even get the chance to mend the puncture. It was the first I'd heard of the puncture. Matt told me the story, and we realised it meant the murder took place soon after Matt left for his game of football."

"I believe you spotted Richard's wallet?" asked Lydia.

"Under the workbench, just outside this door, and to the right."

"Did you realise the gold chain that Eve bought Richard had gone, too?" asked Lydia.

"I couldn't look at Richard's body, Miss," said Harry. "All I could see was the blood."

"Who noticed the bank card was missing?" asked Alex.

"We came back inside when the uniformed people arrived. Two young women, it was, one was a PC, the other was one of those PCSOs or whatever they call them. I noticed the wallet, and the girl marked where it was while Matt was in the office with the other woman. She asked Matt if he could tell if anything was missing. He realised the card had gone."

"Matt phoned the bank to stop the card, didn't he?" asked Alex.

"As soon as we knew it had gone. Someone at the bank told Matt somebody used it the night before."

"Because the balance in the account was low, the killer could only access four hundred pounds," said Alex. "Matt told us you had to wait to get your wages that week."

Harry paused before he replied. Alex knew he was

deciding how much he could afford to say. So Alex didn't press him; he knew Harry would tell the truth in the end.

"We still get customers who prefer to pay in cash these days," said Harry. "Richard had a safe at home. He paid cheques into the firm's bank account, and customers paid by bank transfer. Rather than have cash lying around at the garage, he took it home to store in his safe. If people were late paying their accounts, and that prevented him from transferring our wages into our bank accounts, Richard brought enough cash from his reserves to make us right."

"Because Richard died, and Eve was abroad, there was no way to access the cash," said Alex. "How much might he have had in his reserve, Harry?"

"I couldn't honestly say," said Harry, "but it could have been several thousand pounds, thinking of how many cash payments we'd received during October."

"How often did Richard use the cash reserves to pay your wages?" asked Lydia.

"Once or twice a year," said Harry.

Alex made a note to pass this information on to Gus. Chaloner had been dead for two years. Would HMRC want to hear about it? Harry hinted that Richard didn't record every pound of his income. So how much was there in that safe on Shrivenham Road? Had Eve known how much money was in the safe? Could it have anything to do with the murder?

"What can you tell us about the man in white overalls who arrived here at eleven o'clock on Monday morning?" asked Alex.

"We weren't expecting anyone to bring a vehicle in that morning," said Harry. "We had a car on the forecourt ready for collection and two cars in the workshop. Both were due to be with us until Tuesday mid-morning. I heard this man ask Richard to take a quick look at his van. He had an electrical fault, and he needed to rely on it not cutting out on him. The fault was costing him money. Money he could ill afford to lose."

"How did Richard respond?" asked Lydia.

"Richard told him we had been swamped with work. There was no way we could drop jobs for regular customers. He didn't know whether it would be a quick fix or something that needed hours of work. That made sense to me, but this bloke wasn't happy. I had to get under the car I was working on, and Matt was tuning the engine on the Beemer on the other side. It wasn't possible to hear what they said, but shouting came over the background noise. I slid out from under the car to check if a fight had broken out. It was that heated an argument."

"What did you see?" asked Lydia.

"Nothing," said Harry. "The van had left. Richard was on the phone in the office, checking when the owner of the car on the forecourt was collecting it. So I just got on with what I was doing."

"Richard didn't tell you the van driver's name?" asked Lydia.

"If he had, I would have told the police," said Harry. "Richard didn't mention the incident again."

"Was there any signage on the van to help identify what business this man was in?" asked Alex.

"It was white," said Harry. "All I could see was the windscreen and front grill. He parked the same way your colleague did with her Mini."

"What did you see of the van driver?" asked Alex. "You agreed with the detectives that he was thirty-five to forty-five and wore white overalls. They found an eyewitness on

Ponting Street at around eleven o'clock, who provided the description. The van driver could have been a similar age to Richard. Is it possible they knew one another, and that was why the man believed he could get Richard to help him out?"

"It would be a guess," said Harry, shaking his head. "I didn't stop to make a note of the bloke's details the way one of you would. I was working on a customer's car, which is what I get paid to do. Richard was chatting to the man on the forecourt, and then it got heated when I was under the car. The bloke had gone when I stood up next."

"Who closed the front doors when the rain started?" asked Alex.

"I did," said Harry. "That was after two o'clock, I reckon."

"Had you looked outside between one and two, checking on the weather?"

"I expect I glanced out from time to time; the wind was picking up, and a coke can rattled along the pavement. Finally, I asked Richard if he wanted to close the doors, but he said to hang on until the rain started."

"Did you spot a young lad on the other side of the road?" asked Lydia. "Perhaps he threw away his empty coke can. You know what kids are."

"On the other side of the road?" asked Harry. "No, I can't say I remember seeing anyone."

"Did you know that a man was looking through the garage door window at four o'clock?" asked Alex. "Stan Jones spotted him outside. Only for a minute or two."

"The detective asked me about that coloured chap," said Harry. "If he were one of our regulars, he would have known to come to the side door. But, instead, he must have been a stranger, and I never saw him. We get all sorts here;

it doesn't bother me. I work on British and foreign cars for customers from several continents. I enjoy the variety. No two days are the same."

Lydia thought no day would match Monday, the seventh of November, in 2016.

Chapter Seven

"AS YOU'VE WORKED HERE for so long, Harry, you must know Stan Jones well," said Alex.

"Stan used to bring his old Ford Anglia here when I started working for Richard. That was back in the good old days. Stan's ten years older than me and not in the best of health. He's lost without his wife, poor chap, and his son is never there long enough to realise what a state he's in. So sad, isn't it when your family abandons you?"

"Matt told us young Stan's a long-distance lorry driver," said Alex. "He drives across Europe and the UK."

"I can't remember the last time I saw him," said Harry. "He keeps himself to himself, always has ever since the accident."

"What accident was that?" asked Lydia.

"The lad would have been seven or eight, I suppose," said Harry. "Kids today get involved in Halloween, don't they? Well, Bonfire Night was a big occasion when I was a young boy. Many people today would prefer fireworks were only allowed under controlled conditions. You know, as you see on the banks of the Thames in London on New Year's Eve. They spend an absolute fortune for a few minutes of noise and colour. That spectacle looks great, but it wasn't like that in my day. We had a bonfire on the green, which our parents built from any old rubbish lying around. We children begged and borrowed materials to build a guy, wheeled him around the streets in an old pram, collecting pennies, before getting one father to perch him on top of the bonfire. You might see a dozen rockets, a few Catherine wheels, and Roman candles on the housing estates. Everyone had a sparkler, even the girls. Nobody could afford much more. One year, my dad stood a rocket in a milk bottle and told my brother and me to stand back while he lit the fuse. The milk bottle toppled over, and the rocket flew away six feet off the ground, straight towards a group of people on the far side of the bonfire. They had to scatter to avoid getting hit. Bonfire night could be fun, but it could be dangerous too."

"Did young Stan Jones get hurt in an accident involving fireworks?" asked Alex.

"That was what happened," said Harry. "Not every family shared the community spirit. Kids roamed the streets, letting off crackers and bangers. Anything to annoy the neighbours, especially the elderly, and those with pets."

"Did Stan Jones and his wife join in with the other families on Ponting Street?" asked Lydia.

"I lived on the other side of town before I started working for Richard. I can't say for certain what happened, but young Stan must have watched someone light the fuse on a firework and waited for the flash, but nothing came. So he darted forward and picked it up. It exploded in his face. Stan's left hand and the left-hand side of his face got badly burned."

"How dreadful," said Lydia.

"People said he was a quiet, reserved lad even before the accident," said Harry. "The older kids bullied young Stan when he finally recovered and returned to school. As he's grown older, he's grown a beard to cover parts of the scarring on his face. Stan worked a night shift at one of the local factories until he was twenty and then switched to driving. I suppose it suited him. He could spend hours alone in the cab of his lorry and didn't have to face people."

"A lonely existence," said Alex. "Matt said he wasn't sure whether young Stan had a wife. He didn't recall him ever mentioning grandchildren. Matt didn't know where in the UK young Stan lived. Do you know?"

"If he has a family, he's never brought them here to Ponting Street," said Harry. "Young Stan came home for his mother's funeral. He was alone then and stayed with his father for two weeks. Stan parked the tractor unit for his truck across the road, I remember. How often has he been back since? Hard to tell because it's only ever a flying visit. Young Stan often parks his truck in a lorry park on the A420 and gets a lift into town. He stays one night with his father, two nights at the most, and then he's off again."

"We'll speak to Stan Jones tomorrow," said Alex. "He can fill in the gaps then."

"Would young Stan have known Richard Chaloner, Harry?" asked Lydia.

"I don't see why, Miss," said Harry. "There were a good number of years between them, and they lived in different parts of town. Richard's family came from Pinehurst. I think Stan Jones and his wife moved into Ponting Street as soon as they got married. Young Stan would have left school not long before Richard started the garage business. The lad worked nights for a couple of years before leaving home;

after that, he became a trucker. So their paths might have crossed; briefly, I suppose."

Alex looked at Lydia, who shrugged.

They had run out of questions for Harry Simpkins.

"We'll let you get on with your day, Harry," said Lydia. "Thanks for being so patient. It's unlikely you or Matt will deliver the silver bullet to blow this case wide open, but Mr Freeman tells us it's small steps in the right direction that will get us to the solution we seek. So you and Matt have pointed us toward our next steps."

"Your boss is an odd character," said Harry. "I sensed Matt struggled to keep his temper in check earlier."

"I've learned so much from Mr Freeman in a brief space of time," said Lydia. "What he teaches isn't in books."

"The man is a legend," said Alex. "We haven't found a case he couldn't crack yet."

Alex and Lydia left the office together. Harry strolled along behind. Matt Merchant was explaining something to the young apprentice as they peered at the engine of the Toyota. When he spotted Alex and Lydia, he stood up straight.

"Are we out from under the spotlight now, then?" he asked.

"You were never suspects," said Alex. "Many thanks for letting us use the office. If we need to come back for further information, our colleague DS Sherman will ring you."

Alex slipped into the passenger seat of the Mini and prepared himself for another hair-raising trip along the M4 as they returned to the Old Police Station office.

"There was one case we didn't solve to Gus's satisfaction," said Lydia. "That Burnside character shot at the Cheney Manor Industrial Estate."

"The red-haired sniper," said Alex. "We thought we had a lead on him, but the heavy mob from London descended on the Hub and our office to whisk away any evidence we'd gathered. That murder appears to be a no-go area for Gus Freeman."

AFTER LEAVING Alex and Lydia at the garage on Ponting Street, Gus Freeman drove via Drake's Way and the A4312 towards Oxford Road. Ten minutes later, he stood in the visitor's car park of Gablecross Police Station. He steeled himself for what lay ahead.

The place was a rabbit warren, and once he'd negotiated Reception, he had to find Raj Sengupta's office. The Detective Inspector was head of cybercrime. If it was easy to find his office, it said little for his chances of keeping the public safe from online scammers.

Gus needn't have worried. While he filled in the wordy visitor's book at Reception, someone phoned Raj. Before Gus had time to collect his lanyard and pass, Raj stood beside him, grinning like a Cheshire cat.

"Good morning, Gus," he said. "Follow me. We're just around the corner."

Gus had visited the Hub at London Road frequently. So he thought he knew what to expect from Raj's domain. Subdued lighting, screens as far as the eye can see, and computer nerds whose behaviour swung from raucous frivolity to frantic bursts of keyboard activity. How wrong he was. All was quiet on the Gablecross front, and not a single person looked up as he followed Raj to his office.

"You wished to speak to me about the Chaloner case?" he asked.

"You were the SIO, Raj," said Gus. "What can you tell me?"

"Tom Spencer attended the murder scene and the autopsy," said Raj. "I paid a brief visit to the garage to get a feel for the case. The theft of the money and jewellery were a strong indication it started as a robbery. My guess was Chaloner resisted. There would have been plenty of hand tools in the workshop he might have grabbed. The killer panicked and shot Chaloner. I doubt the employees could be certain whether any hand tools on the premises were in a different place from where they left them the previous evening."

"There were no signs of a struggle," said Gus.

"My point exactly," said Raj. "Chaloner grabbed for a weapon, got shot and fell to the ground."

"What did you make of the punctured bicycle tyre?"

"It kept Chaloner at the garage," said Raj.

"How did you expect Tom Spencer to find the killer?"

"I told him to arrange house-to-house enquiries on Ponting Street. I expected someone to have seen something suspicious."

"You found a witness on Ponting Street at the right time. He described the driver of the white van arguing with Richard Chaloner. A man roughly the same age as Chaloner. Can you recall the witness's name?"

"Two years is a long time, Gus," said Raj.

"We found Ralph Robinson, tucked away in the appendix of the murder file handed to me by the Chief Constable. Can you explain that?"

"I was told to bury it by a senior officer at this station, Gus," said Raj. "Robinson was looking for a woman."

"The TV documentary claiming prostitution was on the increase again in the Manchester Road and Commercial

Road area had got under the skin of the great and good of the town," said Gus. "They told everyone what a pleasant place Swindon was to visit for business and pleasure. Then, the well-publicised double murder earlier in the year and Richard Chaloner's death. It wouldn't have looked good if Ralph Robinson's name and what he was up to appeared in the press. Didn't it dawn on you that the white van man could have been the killer? If Tom Spencer had pursued that man's identity with the same diligence as you took burying a witness, we needn't be reviewing the case."

"We did the best we could with the information we had," said Raj Sengupta. "The top brass wanted a result. Tom was getting nowhere, and then suddenly CCTV caught a theft almost on the garage's forecourt. It was one of several catalytic converter thefts that occurred over weeks. I convinced Tom it was the logical course of action. He threw our limited resources into finding the car thieves."

"Why did you have limited resources?" asked Gus.

"We were three weeks into the murder investigation. I was off work every few days with migraine headaches, and we'd got no breaks. My boss reduced the size of my team by a third. Two weeks later, we switched focus altogether. Tom Spencer joined a team investigating hate crime attacks while I transferred to cybercrime. It was most unsatisfactory. I wanted to end my time as SIO with a win."

Gus thought that was a tall order, given the time the man had spent in the field.

"It might not be too late to salvage something from the wreckage," said Gus. "We'll keep digging for clues. The catalytic converter thefts were nothing to do with that garage. It's possible other cowboy outfits around Swindon handled stolen goods, but Richard Chaloner wasn't among them. I assume you're busy, Raj, so I won't take up any more of your time. It's hard to tell, though. How can you work in such silence? I'd forever be thinking my staff were asleep."

Gus left the office before Raj Sengupta could reply. The Chief Constable had been right in his assessment. Raj was in a better place these days and couldn't harm any ongoing criminal investigations.

As he made the return journey to the Old Police Station office, he wondered what the others had discovered.

LUKE SHERMAN HAD BEEN busy while the rest of the team was interviewing in Swindon. He chased DS Tom Spencer halfway across North Wiltshire and traced the detective to a farm outside Lyneham. Tom agreed to meet with Luke at Gablecross first thing in the morning. Once that was out of the way, Tom could resume his hunt for those responsible for the agricultural machinery thefts.

Luke thought Gus could send someone else for that meeting if that was how the wind was blowing. Perhaps he shouldn't have mentioned the West Mercia job. Ever since he had, Luke sensed Gus was shoving him to the sidelines.

Luke tried to push his feelings of unease into the background. He needed to concentrate on the other task Gus had suggested. Who had a motive to kill Richard Chaloner? What event from the past were they missing? What was it that prompted someone to walk into the garage two years ago and shoot him in the chest?

Social media was a dead end. Luke couldn't find evidence that Richard Chaloner had ever opened an account on any major sites. So Luke dug deeper, wondering whether dating sites were Richard's thing. Chaloner hadn't married until he was forty-four, but he was far from being a loner. On the contrary, he was a social animal. Luke hunted for Richard's name in local press reports. That proved more successful. Adverts appeared from the turn of the century, but the business attracted no bad press.

Luke couldn't find a single disgruntled customer who felt Chaloner had overcharged them for work carried out. None of the local authority departments had ever inspected the premises and found issues that ended with a fine or a day in court. Then, Luke spotted a charity event for the local hospital Richard had sponsored. Luke shook his head; the guy was a saint. It was hopeless.

Blessing Umeh and Neil Davis were the first to return to the fold. As they exited the lift, Luke could tell they felt their trip had been worthwhile.

"I sense you got something new from Eve Chaloner," he said. "Do tell."

"We have an excellent description of the gold chain," said Neil, "but that wasn't the real gem."

"Careful, Neil," said Luke. "You'll crack a genuine joke one day."

Blessing came to Neil's rescue. It was only fair; he'd left her the best bit to tell Luke.

"Eve Chaloner told us Richard was involved in three organisations where he could have formed a connection with the man in the white van."

"I've struggled to find Richard online," said Luke. "Before you got back, I was trying to see whether he appeared in the local press. Nothing so far that would lead to someone wanting him dead. So what was he involved in?"

"The Round Table," said Blessing, "CAMRA, and a Folk Club in Highworth."

"That's terrific," said Luke. "We can take one each and

start hunting for press reports and potential flash points. I can go back to the social media sites now. Those organisations are certain to have an online presence. Richard might not have opened a personal account, but if he were an active member, his name would appear, not highlighted, in items posted."

"The local branches of CAMRA and the Round Table could have a sizeable membership," said Neil. "but I imagine the Folk Club would be the easiest to tackle first, to eliminate it."

"Don't be too hasty," said Blessing. "The person we're looking for could be like Richard Chaloner and belong to all three."

"Good point, Blessing," said Neil. "Can you set the ball rolling, Luke? First, we'll update the Freeman Files with the account of our interview with Eve Chaloner, and then we'll pick up whichever thread you wish."

"That sounds a good plan, Neil," said Luke.

THANKS TO LYDIA'S heavy right foot, she and Alex weren't long behind Blessing and Neil returning to the office. They, too, wanted to get their files updated before committing to anything new. While Alex was in the restroom fetching coffee for everyone, Lydia told the others what they discovered when they first arrived in Ponting Street.

"Matt Merchant looked ready to punch Gus on the nose," she laughed. "We could tell yesterday that Gus didn't believe the catalytic converter thefts had anything to do with Richard Chaloner's garage. He thought it was the quickest way to resolve the issue. He left for Gablecross soon after."

"What were the highlights of your interviews?" asked Blessing.

Alex returned with the coffees, and Lydia waited until everyone was ready.

"Matt Merchant thought the driver of the white van was at least an acquaintance of Chaloner's," she said. "He told us he'd reflected on the day of the murder and decided they weren't total strangers. But, unfortunately, the van driver didn't attend the wedding, so we need to look elsewhere for the connection."

"We've got ideas on that," said Neil.

"Matt reckoned the young lad on the pavement across the road between one and two was more likely to be a drug dealer than anything else. He's used to seeing strange young faces in the area. Matt said it's people who travel from London and spill out from the railway station looking for vulnerable targets."

"Matt could be right," said Luke. "Once you eliminate the possibility of an organised crime gang and the theft of valuable car parts, the younger faces don't fit the back story. Anyone with a beef with Chaloner would be close to his age or older. He didn't come into contact with many people in their early twenties at either of the clubs or societies he'd joined."

"We learned more about Stan Jones, the other neighbour on our list of interviewees," said Alex. "He's been a widower for several years, but he has a son, also called Stan, who drops by once in a blue moon."

"Young Stan's a trucker," said Lydia. "He drives here there and everywhere in this country and Europe, according to Matt Merchant."

"What hid Harry Simpkins have to say?" asked Neil.

"Everything Harry told us tallied with Matt Merchant's account of the day of the murder," said Alex. "He gave the same story for the first stage of the investigation and

Richard's relationship with Eve. One thing differed, but I can't see how it could lead to Chaloner's murder. The house on Shrivenham Road had a safe which Chaloner used to hide cash they received through the business."

"It's a stretch to say he hid it, Alex," said Lydia. "Harry told us although most clients paid by bank transfer or cheque, there were still those that settled the smaller repair bills in cash. Chaloner could have had a safe installed at the garage, but nobody was on the premises from six at night until eight the following morning, and then a long period at the weekend. Why expose the business to unnecessary risk? When he left to cycle home at night, he took any cash off the premises."

"What happened to the cash?" asked Neil.

"Harry said Richard used it a couple of times each year to pay their wages," said Lydia.

"That was when the firm's bank account didn't have enough funds to allow the money to get transferred in the normal way," explained Alex.

"Hardly a killing offence," said Neil. "Did Harry see any of the unidentified persons?

"He saw the white van man," said Alex, "but couldn't add much to what we knew. Harry didn't see the young lad. He knew more about Stan Jones's son, though."

Lydia was explaining what happened to young Stan when he was seven or eight years old when they heard the lift return to the ground floor.

"Just after one o'clock," said Neil. "Gus is on his way. Let's park what we've gathered so far, hear what he has to say, and then give him the highlights of what we've learned."

Nobody had an alternative course of action, so they sat and watched the lift doors.

Gus soon emerged and seemed surprised to see everyone had beaten him back to the office.

"Speeding again, Lydia?" he asked.

"Only a little, guv," she replied.

"Was there any coffee in the pot when the last person left the restroom?" asked Gus.

"I was last to use it, guv," said Alex. "I'll fetch your coffee."

"Thanks, Alex, I need it," said Gus. "I scored one from two this morning. I eliminated the possibility the catalytic converter thefts had anything to do with Richard Chaloner and the garage...."

"We heard that, guv," said Blessing. "Lydia said you almost got a bloody nose."

"I'm light on my feet for a man of my age, Blessing. Anyway, my cunning plan worked. Sadly. Raj Sengupta added nothing good to what we already knew. The man was a liability. He buried Ralph Robinson's name because it didn't suit the picture of Swindon the brochures painted."

"The picture where the only red lights were on the traffic lights, guv," said Neil.

"That's the one, Neil," said Gus. "I don't know who to blame most. Raj spent half of the first weeks of the investigation off sick with migraine headaches. They're not much fun, I grant you, but why didn't the top brass stick someone else in to help Tom Spencer? The poor devil had to carry the burden alone. When the CCTV episode dropped in his lap, Sengupta clung to it as a drowning man does to a life raft. Although it wasn't the right lead to follow, the top brass didn't know that at the time. What did they do? Took one-third of the team off the Chaloner case and assigned them to other duties. Two weeks later, the entire investigation stuttered to a halt. What did they expect? It's the same as the

Chief Constable taking everyone except Alex away from me this afternoon and asking me on Friday why we haven't got a result."

Alex had returned with a black coffee. Gus sighed and took a sip.

"Right, I've got that off my chest. Now, who wants to go first?"

The room fell silent as Lydia recounted the tale they'd heard from Harry Simpkins.

"That poor boy," said Blessing.

"He's a grown man now, Blessing," said Luke.

"We're meeting his father tomorrow," said Gus. "We can broach the matter then."

"I caught up with Tom Spencer, guv," said Luke. "He agreed to report to Gablecross in the morning. We can speak with him there before he dashes back to the countryside chasing tractor thieves."

"Well done, Luke. Do you want to see that through to its conclusion? If you can get to Gablecross for nine o'clock, we'll divide the other interviews between the rest of us."

"Who do you want with you tomorrow, guv," asked Neil.

"We'll meet here first," said Gus. "I'll drive to Ponting Street with Lydia, keeping to the speed limit throughout. We'll interview Stan Jones and then locate Ralph Robinson. Did we get his address, Luke?"

"Farnborough Road, guv," said Luke. "That's near the Coate Water Country Park. I've sent the full details through to you."

"Thanks, Luke. Coate Water, eh, very nice too," said Gus. "I'm not sure how long we'll be with Mr Robinson, but Mrs Fryer will be home by one o'clock. Catherine is still working the morning shifts at the care home. We should get back here from Ponting Street by three o'clock."

"What should the rest of us concentrate on, guv?" asked Alex.

"I'm sure locating Tom Spencer wasn't Luke's only achievement this morning," said Gus. "Also, each of us has a report to update in the Freeman Files. I suggest we use the rest of the afternoon to get those reports together. If we have time, we can then discuss what we've learned and decide whether it alters our plans."

"Do you think tomorrow's interview schedule needs to change, guv?" asked Luke.

"Not a chance," said Gus.

Chapter Eight

GUS COMPLETED his reports for the files and looked to see how the others were progressing.

"Are we ready for a catch-up before the close of play?" he asked.

"I didn't have as much to record as the others, guv," said Luke, "so I started the search for the van driver among members of the organisations Blessing and Neil uncovered. The Swindon Folk Club has been going for almost sixty years and has over five hundred people on its Facebook page. Branch 25 of the Round Table lists a similar number, but the Campaign for Real Ale is less popular. So we thought we could divide the work between three of us to dig out lists of member names."

"I'm ready to help with that, guv," said Neil.

"Me too, guv," added Blessing.

"Will it take long to whittle the numbers down to find people on more than one list who might fit our description?" asked Gus.

"I suggest we use the Hub's facilities if we want speedy

access to membership lists, guv," said Lydia. "Divya will be happy to help. Once she's secured those names, we can ask her to isolate white males between thirty-five and forty-five. Privacy settings vary on Community pages and the like. I discovered that when we were searching for links to Maddy Mills. One of us might have to apply to join the organisation to gain access to the information we need."

"That makes sense," said Gus. "Kenneth Truelove would approve us deferring to his experts. Call Divya and set it up, Luke, and we'll spend the rest of the afternoon debriefing everything we've unearthed today. Alex, Neil, and Blessing will stay in the office tomorrow morning. I don't know how speedy a response will be from the Hub. If you're sitting on your hands for an extended period after I leave the office, I suggest you pick one site, say the Real Ale brigade, and tackle the problem in an old-fashioned way. Call the most prominent name you can find and tell him it's vital he helps the police in their enquiries."

When the team left the office at five o'clock, everyone knew what they had to do tomorrow. They had made tentative forward steps in the investigation today, but there could be a long way to go before it ended successfully.

As Gus heard the lift descending to the ground floor, his phone buzzed. He had a message from Suzie. She had just left London Road and was driving to the Great Western Hospital near Junction 15 on the M4 to visit Vicky Bennison.

Gus tidied his desk and followed the others. Once in the car park, he reversed the Focus out of the only occupied parking space reserved for the Crime Review Team and headed home. The cooler weather was welcome, and as he passed the London Road HQ on his way to the bungalow in Urchfont, Gus let his mind drift over the events of the day.

The vague notion that formed in the Chief Constable's office yesterday lunchtime was still valid. Although he'd annoyed Matt Merchant by suggesting Richard Chaloner was a crook, it had cleared one motive for the murder off the table. Moreover, the reports of the interviews he'd read with Matt Merchant, Harry Simpkins, and Eve Chaloner added credence to his insistence that the killing was personal. As for the time he'd spent with Raj Sengupta, that proved beyond doubt the original investigation lacked leadership and direction. Tom Spencer had been working in the dark, blindfolded and with one hand tied behind his back. Luke wouldn't gain much new information tomorrow morning.

As he turned into the gateway of the bungalow, Gus made a mental note to chat with Luke sooner rather than later. Geoff Mercer had warned him West Mercia liked to conclude matters quickly. If he let himself get distracted, the team could lose one of its key members. Why was life so difficult?

Gus stood in the hallway for a moment to clear his head. How long would Suzie get to spend with Vicky if she was still poorly? He glanced at the clock. It was twenty minutes to six. Suzie would have reached the hospital five minutes ago. He could tackle two or three tasks that would earn him brownie points before preparing their meal. Suzie would be home by half-past seven at the latest.

When Gus heard her VW Golf rattle through the gateway at twenty past seven, he had hoovered and dusted and loaded the washing machine with discarded clothing and damp towels. His efforts in the kitchen had produced a nutritious vegetable and bacon frittata ready to serve.

"Welcome home, sweetheart," said Gus as Suzie came through the front door.

"Oh, Gus," sighed Suzie. She dropped her handbag by the hall table and flung her arms around his neck.

"That was dreadful," she said. "Vicky's a little better today, but nothing prepares you for those wires and cuts and bruises around her face. That swine did a number on the poor woman. I could sit with Vicky for thirty minutes. It should have been fifteen, but Divya's husband, Arjun, persuaded the senior staff nurse to let me stay a while longer."

"I'm glad Vicky's improving," said Gus. "Let's hope she's over the worst. What could Arjun tell you regarding the bleed on the brain?"

"Nothing, as I'm not a relative," said Suzie. "But, when the nurses were out of earshot, he assured me Vicky's life was no longer in danger. What can I hear?"

"The washing machine in the utility," said Gus. "I needed to keep busy while I waited for you to get home. Dinner's ready as soon as you are."

"It smells delicious," said Suzie. "Let's eat, and then I'm looking forward to a quiet night in front of the telly."

"After the day we've both had," said Gus, "It's the least we deserve."

Wednesday, 5 September 2018

LUKE SHERMAN LEFT home at half-past seven. The drive to Gablecross Police Station would take the best past of ninety minutes from Warminster. Nicky was still sleeping when Luke got up to go to the bathroom.

Last night had been the same as most nights of late. Nicky asked when he would decide on the job change; Luke told him a sideways move wasn't what his career needed. Nicky got angry, accusing Luke of not caring how the long hours affected their relationship, and when they went to bed, nothing had been resolved.

Luke arrived at Gablecross, signed in, and followed the signs to where the detective squad lived. He had visited the building on several occasions and spotted a familiar face on the far side as he entered the large room.

"Good morning, Jake. Any sign of Tom Spencer this morning?"

"Luke, how's it going, mate," said DS Jake Latimer. "Neil Davis let you come alone, did he? How is the reprobate, anyway? He sounded stressed the other day when he gave me a bell."

"Neil's fine, and Melody is still pregnant," said Luke. "For which they're both grateful."

"I'm still with the same girl," said Jake. "Wonders will never cease, but we're not following Neil and Melody's example. Not yet anyway. I know why you're here, Luke. Neil told me Gus Freeman got the short straw and collected the Richard Chaloner murder file. Tom Spencer won't be long. He's a good lad, steady if not spectacular. My money would be on him running down those tractor thieves in time. He's like a dog with a bone. Here he comes now."

Luke thanked Jake Latimer and turned to greet DS Tom Spencer.

Tall, dark, and handsome didn't entirely cover it. Luke hadn't expected that.

"You must be Luke Sherman," said Tom. "My desk is over the other side. Let's get this done, and I can drive to Great Somerford. I found a lead late yesterday afternoon that could tie up the case I'm on."

Tom flopped into his chair and pointed to the one beside him.

"Take the weight off, Luke. What was it you wanted to know?"

"Gus Freeman spoke to the SIO, DI Sengupta, yesterday morning," said Luke.

"So I heard," said Tom. "The Chaloner case was not our finest hour. We would have done things differently if I had been in charge, but it's water under the bridge now. The house-to-house collected several useful pieces of information, but we never got to sixty percent of the people living on the street. I told Raj if they weren't there during the day, it was because they were at work. What was the point of going back the next morning? We should have visited Ponting Street between six and seven in the evening to catch more residents at home. That was the time the murder took place on Monday night. I thought witnesses would remember things more clearly when the conditions were similar, even if it wasn't bucketing with rain."

"Gus heard you wanted to spread the house-to-house wider," said Luke. "What was the thinking there?"

"The two incidents in the afternoon felt odd," said Tom. "We only asked people living in houses on Ponting Street whether they saw someone hanging around looking suspicious. What was so special about that street? If they were housebreakers or opportunist thieves, they would have visited several streets seeking targets. Raj got hung up on it being a robbery gone wrong and insisted the van driver who had the stand-up row with Chaloner was our chief suspect. I wanted to get more data to be sure we were on the right path. Whenever I got back here and went to his office to ask if we could change tack, he had gone home. I asked a couple of his colleagues what I should do. They asked why I was questioning what the SIO had told me to do. Who did I think I was? So, I carried on the hunt for the three persons of interest we identified until Raj returned to work. The next thing I know, he's got a bee in his bonnet over catalytic converters, and there's a complete change of direction. I'm talking to detectives working on cases involving criminal gangs. They didn't want to waste time with me and had never heard of Richard Chaloner and Ponting Street. The team shrunk as soon as we changed tack, and after chasing half a dozen false trails, Raj told me his boss wanted us to shelve the case. There was little likelihood of it ever showing a positive outcome."

"Did Raj interview Ralph Robinson?" asked Luke.

"No, I spoke to him. That was a waste of time. No sooner had I dropped the report onto Raj's desk than he told me to bury it."

"We understand why that happened," said Luke. "There's no excuse, but what was Robinson's story, anyway?"

"Robinson told his wife he was off to South Marston. Both his parents had died several years before, and Ralph went there to lay flowers on the grave. That day, Ralph drove in the opposite direction and parked at the far end of Ponting Street. Then he walked past Chaloner's garage on his way to a house on the other side of Manchester Road. Ponting Street is one of several streets that bisects the popular but notorious highway."

"I didn't realise," said Luke. "I must remember to study the street map on our office wall more closely. So, Ralph Robinson knew somebody living on the stretch of Ponting Street closer to the railway station?"

"Yes, a lady called Jane Kimble, who answered to the name Mistress Quickly. She greeted her gentleman callers at the door dressed as a comely maiden from the time of Henry the Fourth and regaled them with monologues from the Bard during their stay. It takes all sorts."

"Henry the Fourth, Part One and Two," said Luke. "That was where Mistress Quickly featured, wasn't it? Perhaps the Merry Wives of Windsor too."

"Don't ask me, Luke," said Tom. "We didn't study Shakespeare at my school. Although I don't believe Jane Kimble offered a Part Two on her tariff, she insisted on a rapid turnover of clients. She's hung up her costume now and qualifies for her bus pass next year. When pressed, Ralph Robinson admitted they used to go to primary school together."

"Their liaison hadn't been going on that long, had it?" asked Luke.

"I don't know the full history, Luke," said Tom. "Jake Latimer told me Jane was into amateur dramatics. After her time as a leading lady passed, she found a part she could play that provided an income. I suspect, from what Jake said, that Jane set up in business around the time Ralph lost his parents."

"Two trips a year to the cemetery at South Marston," said Luke. "The flowers were for Jane. I should warn Gus Freeman. He's seeing Ralph at his home later this morning."

"It might be fun to pass on what I told you and let the interview play out in front of his wife," said Tom. "It was Ralph Robinson who saw the driver of the white van arguing the toss with Chaloner at around eleven o'clock. As he strolled along Ponting Street with his bunch of flowers, Ralph had a splendid view of what was happening on the forecourt. He gave us our only decent description of the man in the white overalls."

"Did you ask whether he knew the man?" asked Luke.

"Of course," said Tom. "Ralph said he thought he was a painter and decorator."

"He didn't need to know him to guess what he did for a living," said Luke.

"Ralph told me he didn't know his name," said Tom. "I suppose if Ralph had lived and worked in Swindon throughout his life, he recognised hundreds of people by sight without ever learning their name."

"What did you make of Stan Jones?" asked Luke.

"That was the old chap who saw the man peering through the garage window, wasn't it? I visited him in the afternoon, hoping to prove he could have been wrong about what he said he saw. But, unfortunately, your eyesight can fool you when the light is fading, and it's raining. Besides, Stan Jones isn't in the best of health. He's hard of hearing and often forgets where he's put his glasses. So I didn't think he was a reliable witness."

"Did you ask Stan if he'd seen the van driver?" asked Luke.

"Well, it was light, and it hadn't yet rained," said Tom. "If I'd asked him that question, Stan might have given us a more detailed description. But, no, I didn't ask. The uniforms did the house-to-house. I passed the results to DI Sengupta. He told us to go back on Wednesday morning to check those addresses that didn't answer the door the night before. So that's what they did. Raj didn't suggest we asked a different set of questions of the people who had initially given us our three persons of interest."

"It might have helped," said Luke. "Mrs Fryer worked the morning shift at the care home. She said a young lad was hanging around on the pavement outside her house for an hour. Apart from popping out to post a letter, Mrs Fryer was home for the rest of the afternoon. Why didn't someone ask her whether she saw what Stan Jones witnessed? Mrs Fryer might have known the person looking through the window or at least given a better description to enable you to speak to him. Mrs Fryer could have seen the car registration or noticed the girl driving the car and described her. Jake says you're a methodical detective, Tom, but surely you can see you let a few opportunities slip through your fingers?"

"With the benefit of hindsight, yes, you're right, Luke. I said it wasn't our finest hour. Is there anything else you think I missed? Let's get it out in the open, and I can reach Great Somerford before the thieves have got those tractors into a container and on their way to Eastern Europe."

"Did Stan Jones mention his son during your visit?" asked Luke.

"He never stopped saying how much he missed his wife since she died," said Tom. "You know what people Stan's age can be like. They rabbit on, telling you their life story when you want to home in on five minutes from a specific day."

"Hang on," said Luke. "Was Stan talking about his wife or his son's wife? His only child's name is Stan too. He's a long-distance lorry driver. We've heard he rarely visits Ponting Street because of his job and moved away from Swindon around fifteen years ago."

"That's news to me," said Tom. "Stan could have got confused. His wife died several years ago. I checked, and I'm sure he misses her. Stan's alone in that house twenty-four seven. I'm trying to recall the actual words he used. He told me how much he missed his wife, and then he said–'He missed her just like me. They were so happy, both of them, as happy as we had been. But, then, before you know it, it's over. You don't know what heartbreak is until something like that happens to you.' I let him ramble on and tried to get him to focus on the window and what he saw on Monday afternoon, but it was hopeless. Raj wasn't at work for a day or two after that, and when he returned, I told him I didn't believe Stan Jones was a reliable witness. I didn't know he could have been talking about his son as well as himself."

"It could be irrelevant," said Luke. "We don't know the son's whereabouts. Young Stan visited his father on odd occasions, but they aren't close. There's nothing to suggest he knew Richard Chaloner, anyway."

"I'm sure you'll clarify matters when you speak to Ralph Robinson and Stan Jones," said Tom. "I imagine you're calling on Mrs Fryer, too. I wish you well. Can I leave now?"

"If I think of anything else, I have your number," said Luke.

"I've only got your office number," said Tom Spencer with a grin. "If you give me your mobile number, perhaps we can go for a drink sometime?"

Luke's mouth suddenly felt dry. Something else he hadn't expected.

"I'm engaged," said Luke. "We haven't set a date yet."

"Good," said Tom. "That means there's still hope."

GUS FREEMAN HAD ARRIVED at the Old Police Station car park as Luke Sherman was parking his car at Gablecross. Neil wasn't far behind him, and the other three team members made it upstairs to the office a minute before nine o'clock.

"Will this outfit be too much for a man in his seventies, guv?" asked Lydia.

"It would be too much for many men several years younger, Lydia," said Gus.

Gus knew Lydia could never permanently tame her wild, red hair, and today she'd given up the fight. Her multi-coloured summer blouse made him wish he hadn't left his sunglasses in the Focus. At least the black skirt was a mid-calf length, and her kitten-heeled boots only had a moderate three-inch heel.

Gus decided they could dispense with a defibrillator when they visited Stan Jones this morning.

"We'll get going then," he said. "Is everyone clear on what they're doing?"

"Yes, guv," said Neil. "I've never tried Real Ale this early in the day, but needs must."

Gus and Lydia were already on their way to the lift.

"What are you hoping to learn from these three inter-views, guv?" asked Lydia. "I appreciate you asking me to tag along today, but what's my role?"

"We'll play it by ear with Stan Jones," said Gus. "I want more detail on the man who visited the garage at four o'clock. It might be unwise to discount him as having any involvement in the murder. My initial thoughts were that the killer acted alone, but I've been wrong before."

"The man and woman could have been accomplices," said Lydia. "His role was to keep watch, and the girl slashed the bicycle tyre. That's plausible, but if murder is personal, surely it restricts the number of people involved, doesn't it? Or is that too simplistic?"

"One man can be the target for many people who have a motive for getting of him," said Gus. "We have yet to identify the true motive behind Chaloner's murder. We only discard people from our investigation once we've proved beyond any doubt they weren't involved."

"Are you considering a change of car, guv?" asked Lydia as she opened the Focus's passenger door.

"It gets me from A to B, Lydia," said Gus. "That's good enough for me for the immediate future. We wouldn't have time to chat about the case if you were driving. My heart would be in my mouth, which tends to restrict my ability to carry on a conversation."

"I wonder how Luke is getting on at Gablecross," asked Lydia.

Gus didn't reply. He was hoping Luke wasn't counting down the days before he drove to London Road to discuss an impending transfer to the Midlands with Geoff Mercer.

Gus parked the Focus outside Stan Jones's terraced house at a quarter past ten. Matt Merchant and his two employees were hard at work in the garage across the road.

Matt spotted Gus and nodded a tentative greeting. Lydia rang the doorbell on the weathered wooden front door and then waited for the homeowner to answer. The door edged open halfway.

"What do you want?" asked Stan Jones. "I'm expecting the police any minute. Clear off."

"We are the police," said Lydia. "Here's my card. Mr Freeman here is my boss."

"You had better come in," said Stan. "You didn't look like any police officer I've met."

"Ms Barre is a plain clothes detective," said Gus, tongue firmly in cheek as Stan led them into a dark, depressing front room.

Gus had visited hundreds of similar properties over the years. Two-up, two-down had served many families well in Victorian times. If they saw the rest of the property, they would find a kitchen and utility room at the rear, with two bedrooms and a bathroom upstairs. To make up for the lack of a front garden, there would be a long narrow strip of land at the rear useful for many things: a small garden shed, a vegetable plot, and a patch of grass for rare moments of leisure time. Today, it needed to house several bins for waste and recycling.

Stan sat in his chair by the window. Gus and Lydia perched on a worn sofa. When the uniformed officers sat here during the house-to-house, they would have accepted that Stan had a decent view of the garage from that chair. When he told them he saw an Afro-Caribbean man, between twenty-five and thirty years of age, peering through the window, it wouldn't have seemed odd.

Those interviews took place on Tuesday evening. The heavy velour curtains would have been closed, and the over-head light switched on. The TV may well have been on in the corner to Gus's right, illuminating the room, even if Stan had muted the sound.

This morning, in early September, with the curtains drawn back as far as they would go, the street on this side was still in shadow. The living room was dark, and the grey net curtains at the window didn't improve matters. At four o'clock on a wet November afternoon, Stan Jones might have been mistaken. Not about the ethnicity of the person he saw, but the age range.

"We'd like to run through the statement you made to the police two years ago," said Gus. "Do you remember what that related to, Mr Jones?"

"I'd forgotten about it until someone rang me the other day," said Stan. "He reminded me that I spoke to a young person in uniform and then a detective. It was when Mr Chaloner died across the road. Nothing like that had ever happened in this neighbourhood. Jeanie and I moved here when we got married, raised our son, and even after cancer took her from me too soon, I'd never felt in any danger."

"Murder is rare," said Gus. "You told the police you saw a man looking through the garage window at four o'clock. How could you be sure of the time?"

"I was watching the horse racing on the box, and the four o'clock at Newcastle had just got underway."

"Had you backed a runner?" asked Gus.

Stan's laugh quickly became a harsh cough.

"Not on my pension."

"What made you look out of the window?"

"A sudden movement. A black bloke was jumping up and down over the road. He was trying to see inside the garage."

"Had you been sat there all afternoon?" asked Gus.

"I've got nowhere else to be," said Stan. "These arthritic hips of mine are worse in cold, damp weather."

"Why were you so certain he was in his twenties?" asked Lydia.

"Is that what I said?" asked Stan.

"You described his clothing as dark, and he looked to be between twenty-five and thirty," said Gus.

"Everyone dresses alike, don't they? I reckon he wore jeans, trainers, and a dark jacket like they all do. It was raining, and he was only there for a minute or two. He had dreadlocks under the striped hat he wore; I remember that. When he jumped up the last time, his hat almost fell off. He was fixing that when the headlights of the car blinded me for a few seconds. A girl picked him up. He ran across the road and got in the passenger side. She stopped there, just past my window. By the time I got out of this chair to see anything, they were gone."

"What made you think it was a girl?" asked Lydia.

"Long dark hair, that's what I saw," said Stan.

"She stopped the car past your window," said Lydia. "So. the only time you saw her was while she slowed after her headlights blinded you?"

"A few seconds at most," said Gus. "Maybe the driver didn't own a striped beanie."

"You've lost me," said Stan.

"The driver could have been another Afro-Caribbean man," said Lydia.

Chapter Nine

GUS WONDERED whether this case was taking another unexpected twist.

Instead of getting Stan Jones to add to their knowledge about the mystery four o'clock visitor, they could have discovered that Stan's eyesight might be unreliable.

To compound that problem, Stan might have opened a new line of enquiry. Why were two Afro-Caribbean males interested in what was going on at Chaloner's garage?

Lydia realised Gus was miles away, and Stan Jones was staring out of the window.

"Do you do a lot of people watching?" she asked.

"It passes the time of day," said Stan.

"It's half-past ten," said Lydia. "Do you fancy a coffee or a cup of tea?"

Stan went to get out of his chair, but Lydia stopped him.

"You sit and chat with Mr Freeman," she said. "I'm a plain clothes detective. If I couldn't find what I need in your kitchen, I wouldn't be much use, would I?"

"A cup of tea for me. Miss, two sugars, please," said Stan.

The conversation brought Gus out of his reverie.

"Stan was looking out of the window, guv," hinted Lydia as she headed for the kitchen.

Gus latched on to what she was driving at.

"Were you sat in your chair in the morning on the day Richard Chaloner died?"

"I expect so," said Stan.

"Harry Simpkins told us there was an argument on the forecourt, close to eleven o'clock. Does that ring a bell?"

"That would have been Eddie Dolman," said Stan. "He's an argumentative beggar."

"What does Eddie do for a living, Stan? Any ideas?" asked Gus, fully alert now.

"A painter and decorator ever since he left school," said Stan. "Eddie comes from Pinehurst."

"The same as Richard Chaloner," said Gus. "Perhaps they were at school together."

"I heard they spent a lot of time together, especially when they were younger," said Stan.

Lydia returned with two coffees and a cup of tea.

"Did you see much of the argument?" asked Gus.

"I saw it, but I didn't hear what they said," said Stan. "Eddie seemed het up over something, but Richard kept his cool, as always. Finally, after several minutes, Eddie got in his van and sped off up the street. I haven't seen him since."

"Where do you eat your lunch, Stan?" asked Lydia.

"I bring it in here on a tray and watch Bargain Hunt, then the news. I don't always watch the whole bulletin if it's boring or if the first race on the other channel is about to start."

"So, it's possible you were sitting here between one and two in the afternoon?" asked Lydia.

"I might have needed the loo," said Stan. "But I would have been here most of the time."

"Do you know Mrs Fryer, one of your neighbours?" asked Gus.

"Of course I know her. Cath got on famously with my Jeanie."

"Cath tells us a young man was standing on the pavement outside her house when she got home from work. Did you see anybody?"

"I can't say I did. Mind you, Cath's house is a few doors away, towards Manchester Road. I wouldn't have seen him unless he walked ten or fifteen yards this way or crossed the street."

"Has your son called on you lately, Stan?" asked Gus.

"He's a busy man, Mr Freeman," said Stan. "He'll drop by when he needs a free bed for the night."

"Where does he live?" asked Gus.

"I don't have an address for him I'm certain of," said Stan. "He rented flats in Swindon after he left home, places that were cheap and near the firm where he worked. Then he changed jobs without a word to us and went truck driving. The further he could get away from this town, the better."

"Why Stan?" asked Lydia.

"You haven't met him, have you?" said Stan.

"We heard about the accident," said Gus.

"That was part of it," said Stan. "He didn't want to watch his mother suffer was another."

"Where's the firm based he works for now?" asked Gus.

"He's an independent trucker," said Stan. "My lad has his own tractor unit. He'll hitch it to whatever needs transporting to anywhere for anybody. All he's interested in is getting on the open road and away from people."

"You're telling us Stan doesn't have a fixed address," said Gus. "He'll sleep in his cab or book into a hotel or motel, in whichever part of the continent he's in."

Stan nodded.

"This is his home address for official stuff," said Stan. "He drops in every few months to pick up his post. I asked him to give me a forwarding address, but he shrugged and said there was no point. He was never in one place long enough to put down roots."

"Stan hasn't married then?" asked Lydia.

"That was the other reason Stan started trucking and moved as far away as he could," said Stan. "She broke his heart."

"The relationship ended," said Lydia. "That must have been dreadful for both of you. Was your wife still alive?"

"Jeanie passed in 2005, but she was ill for a long while before that. Stan moved away from Swindon after he started driving the lorries. He'd had a miserable childhood despite the love we gave him. Kids at school bullied and taunted him. As he grew older and started work, the scarring from the accident faded a little, and Stan grew a beard to hide the worst of it. He met Tara when he was working nights at the factory. A quiet thing she was, but they got on. Stan asked her to marry him, and she said yes. He saved for an engagement ring, and they set a date. I'll never forget the look on Jeanie's face when Stan told her the news. Jeanie was determined to stay with us long enough to see them get married."

"What happened?" asked Lydia.

"We stood in the registry office, waiting, for over an hour," said Stan. "Tara's family was there. It was only Tara and her father who were missing. She couldn't go through with it. Stan was devastated. He couldn't understand what he'd done wrong. The scars on his hand and face hadn't horrified Tara. They'd been seeing one another for two years. That was the start of it. Jeanie went downhill; she gave up the fight. I couldn't help her, nor could I help Stan. He started going on longer trips across Europe and not coming here so often. The only time he stayed with me for more than a couple of days was after Jeanie died."

"How did you contact him?" asked Gus.

"What do you mean?" asked Stan.

"You told us you don't have an address for him. And he spent far longer periods away from Swindon than in the past. So how did he learn his mother had died?"

"It beats me, Mr Freeman," said Stan. "I was in such a state when Jeanie went that it never registered. Stan turned up three or four days after she died and stayed with me until after the funeral. I put a notice in the Advertiser. Maybe he kept in touch that way."

"Have you seen your son this year, Stan?" asked Lydia.

"I must have done, Miss, but don't ask when it was. April perhaps, he likes the Spring."

That made sense thought Gus. It was a popular time of year for official documentation.

So, young Stan got jilted at the altar. An unpleasant experience for a young man who had already suffered more than enough.

"You could have done with Stan being at home when the police were on your doorstep every couple of days, Stan," said Gus.

"I never saw hide nor hair of him after Easter that year, Mr Freeman," said Stan. "It must have been Christmas before his trucking brought him this way again. He leaves his truck in a lorry park on the outskirts and catches a bus into the town centre. Then, when he's ready, he finds his way back here and sleeps in his old bedroom. I always ask him to stay with me for longer, but he says he needs to keep working."

"Thanks for the coffee, Stan," said Gus. "We need to visit someone else now. You've been a great help. We've wanted to name that man arguing with Richard for two years. It's a shame nobody asked you before. As for the two people in the car, the information you added today could prove useful."

Stan Jones followed them to the door and watched Gus and Lydia drive away. He closed the door, and as he returned to his chair, he opened a drawer on the dresser next to the television. Why he'd kept the wedding invitation, he couldn't fathom. Stan wondered what had happened to Tara Laing. She'd never got in touch afterwards in person. Just a sympathy card in the post after Jeanie passed.

Stan sighed and resumed his place next to the window. Things hadn't been the same since Saturday, the eighth of November 2003. If things had been different, he could have had grandchildren running around in this house by now if Stan and Tara had stayed in Swindon.

"Eddie Dolman, guv," said Lydia as they drove towards Ralph Robinson's address. "At last, we've got a genuine lead to follow. How many blokes can there be with dreadlocks in Swindon? Surely, they shouldn't be that hard to find. Why would they be interested in the garage, anyway?"

"I haven't got a clue," said Gus. "It's something to look at this afternoon after we get back to the office. I want to stop before we reach Farnborough Road to call Alex. Now we know the name of the man with the van, we needn't dig into the memberships of those organisations."

"It will be good to get confirmation, guv," said Lydia, "and our two friends from the afternoon visit could turn up on those lists too,"

"I can't see them being into folk music or real ale, Lydia," said Gus.

"Perhaps there's another connection, guv."

As they approached Coate Water, Gus parked in a lay by and called the office. He passed the details to Alex of their conversation with Stan Jones.

Gus was preparing to drive to Ralph Robinson's house when his phone rang.

"Luke," he said. "Everything okay? How was it with Tom Spencer? A waste of time?"

"Not in the slightest, guv," said Luke. "It was most revealing. Are you with Ralph Robinson yet?"

"Half a mile away, Luke, why?"

"Robinson made two trips a year for three or four years to an address in Ponting Street. Tom believed the dates corresponded to the dates his parents died. The lady in question was an old school friend who built a business based on a Shakespearean character."

"You're on speakerphone, Luke," said Gus. "Do I need to cover Lydia's ears?"

Luke told them what he'd learned from Tom Spencer.

"Will you be back in the office soon?" asked Gus.

"In the next twenty minutes, guv," said Luke.

"Alex will bring you up to speed. It's unlikely we'll get back before three. I hope you'll have good news for us by then."

"Intriguing," said Luke. "What a morning I'm having. See you two later."

Gus drove to Farnborough Road and parked outside the address Luke had given him.

Ralph Robinson and his wife lived in a modest, three-bedroom, semi-detached house. At least, Gus presumed the wife was still there. Tom Spencer's revelation had caused a giggle from his passenger, but Raj Sengupta had done his best to keep Ralph's name out of the spotlight.

Gus pressed the doorbell.

"What is that tune?" asked Lydia. "It sounds familiar."

"Edelweiss," said Gus. "A glance at the front garden and the Venetian blinds in the windows suggests nothing much has changed here for decades."

A short, stocky lady with silver hair, wearing a rumpled cardigan and knee-length skirt, opened the door.

"Mrs Robinson?" asked Gus.

The Simon and Garfunkel tune played in his head despite his best efforts. The lady on the doorstep couldn't have been further from the image of the film character.

"Are you the police?" she asked.

"Mr Freeman, a consultant with Wiltshire Police, that's me," said Gus. "My colleague Ms Logan Barre and I are here to speak with your husband."

"Ralph's in the conservatory. Go to the end of the corridor into the kitchen, and you'll find the door open. I won't join you if you don't mind."

"That's fine, Mrs Robinson," said Lydia. "We'll try not to keep him too long."

"It makes no odds to me, love."

With that, Mrs Robinson returned to the lounge and closed the door.

"Happy families," said Lydia as they made their way through the kitchen to the sunlit conservatory beyond.

Gus noted that the rear garden confirmed his view the couple had lived here since they married, and as the marriage soured, so did any care and attention to the decorative order of home and garden.

Ralph Robinson looked every bit of his seventy years, as did his wife. The reason for his spending the mornings in this room was plain. It had the best of any sun, and as he was a heavy smoker, his wife had banished him from the house. Gus thought these days Ralph was lucky not to have to stand in a makeshift shelter outside in all winds and weather.

"Sorry about Betty," said Ralph. "She's a miserable cow, has been for years. Once the kids grew up and moved away, we discovered we had little in common."

"We're not marriage counsellors, Mr Robinson," said Gus. "We need to clarify a few points on the information you gave to the police two years ago. Remind us again what you were doing on Ponting Street that morning."

Ralph Robinson studied Lydia for a second. Lydia stood and closed the door to the kitchen.

"We know the truth, Mr Robinson," she said. "Please don't insult us."

"I told Betty I was taking flowers to put on my mother's grave," said Ralph Robinson, lighting another cigarette. "I was going to see an old friend. I hoped it could become more than a business arrangement between us, but Jane stopped answering my calls after the police spoke to me. Betty suspected I'd been seeing someone but never asked. She wasn't interested. Betty lives her life, and I live mine, what's left of it. These fags will be the death of me within eighteen months to two years, the doctors tell me. Fat chance of giving them up after you've smoked since you were fourteen years old. I'll be better off out of it anyway, the way the world's going."

Happy families indeed, Gus thought. Time to get back to the matter at hand.

"We're interested in what you saw as you made your way from the car to your appointment, Mr Robinson," said Gus.

"An argument outside the garage," said Ralph. "Two men, forty years old maybe, having a slanging match over something of nothing. The man in the overalls wanted his van checked over, and the mechanic refused."

"That mechanic was the garage owner, Richard Chaloner," said Gus. "Someone shot him dead inside the workshop a mere seven hours after that argument."

"I realised that after the news broke," said Ralph. "I'd seen both men in town over the years, but I wasn't on speaking terms with either of them."

"Where might you have seen them?" asked Gus.

"The man with the van worked at properties along this road. I could have approached him to get this place in better order, but he didn't have his name or contact number on his van. So he must have got his business by word of mouth, I suppose. I could have asked someone for his number, but I couldn't be bothered. The other man had his face in the papers from time to time. He always showed people how well he was doing by sponsoring charity events. You know the sort. I'm surprised he didn't stand for the council."

"You didn't see them together at any other functions?" asked Gus. "Did you and your wife belong to any clubs or societies?"

Ralph stubbed out his cigarette.

"Do me a favour. No, that morning was the only time I can recall seeing them together, but I knew their faces.

They'd both lived in Swindon for years, born here, I shouldn't wonder."

"At what time did you return to your car?" asked Lydia.

"Just after twelve," said Ralph. "A maximum of an hour was what Jane allowed."

"The van driver had left the garage by then?" asked Gus.

"Someone was moving a car from the workshop onto the forecourt, and the man I saw earlier was taking another car inside. But, apart from that, the street was empty, except for the odd car driving through."

Gus couldn't see Ralph Robinson adding anything valuable to what they already knew. He could tell Lydia was uncomfortable with the smoky atmosphere, despite the open windows in the conservatory. He'd grown up with the smell as his parents both smoked. Just like Ralph Robinson, the habit had taken them to an early grave.

"Thank you for your time, Mr Robinson," said Gus. "Don't get up. We'll find our way out. We won't disturb your wife either."

Ralph Robinson lit another cigarette and picked up his newspaper. Lydia led the way outside, and Gus closed the front door firmly behind them. As they walked to the car, Lydia shook herself.

"I wish we could stop in Chippenham, guv. I want to go home to shower and change clothes. How can people live that way?"

"We can make the detour after we've dropped by Cath Fryer's place, Lydia," said Gus. "I told Luke we wouldn't get back until three. Robinson was as much use as a chocolate teapot as far as giving us any little gems he'd kept hidden two years ago. A pathetic individual who will stay on the fringes of this case. We won't need to return here, thank goodness."

Cath Fryer had been home for ten minutes when Gus parked on Ponting Street for the second time that day. A jolly woman in her early fifties, she welcomed them into her home like long-lost friends. The difference between the Robinson and Fryer households couldn't have been more marked.

"We're earlier than we thought," said Gus. "I hope that hasn't inconvenienced you, Mrs Fryer."

"That's alright," she replied. "Mr Freeman, wasn't it? I think that was the name the young man gave when he rang. Who are you then, my dear, another police officer?"

"Ms Logan Barre," said Lydia. "What a lovely house you have."

"We try, my dear," said Cath. "My husband did most of the work on the house himself, and he's a keen gardener. I work in Dean Park in the mornings. Then, in the afternoons, I potter in the garden at this time of year. Dave can put his feet up in the evening."

"You still work at the care home then, Mrs Fryer?" asked Gus.

"Oh yes, it's where Dave's mother went after his father died. I started volunteering years ago, and they offered me a part-time job. When the kids were young, I stayed at home, but I needed something to keep me busy when they flew the nest. I don't enjoy sitting around."

"We've spoken to several people about the events surrounding Richard Chaloner's death," said Gus. "You told the police you saw a young man outside your house, wearing a bomber jacket. His behaviour made you suspicious of his intentions."

"That's right," said Cath. "What can I say? He was there when I came home. He didn't budge when I tried to pass him on the pavement, and he hadn't moved an inch when I came out again with a letter to take to the post box. An hour, just hanging around. I didn't like the look of the lad."

"Was he a stranger?" asked Gus.

"I'd never seen him before and never saw him again after that day."

"It was November, so I don't expect you were pottering in the garden later that afternoon," said Gus.

"Oh no, dear, I watch Christmas films on television in the afternoons during November. They're always soppy and sentimental, and Dave wouldn't watch them with me, but after a morning at the care home, sometimes I just need to take my mind off things."

"Did you see anyone else in the street that afternoon?" asked Gus. "Anyone across the road at the garage, perhaps?"

"The film hadn't long started when I had to switch on the light in this front room," said Cath. "The skies got very dark, and the next time I looked out, it was raining hard. Someone had closed the garage doors. The lights were still on, Richard and his men were working inside. As I closed the curtains to shut out the awful weather, I saw a man looking into the garage window. He had to stand on tiptoe."

"Can you describe him?" asked Lydia.

"A Rastafarian," said Cath, "wearing one of those floppy hats."

"Had you seen him before?" asked Gus.

"I don't think so, my dear, but he wasn't there long. I thought he was trying to attract the attention of someone inside. Why he didn't go to the side door, I don't know.

Then, it started raining harder, and someone picked him up. A car drove past slowly and parked further along the street."

"Outside Stan Jones's house," said Gus. "Yes, he told us this morning."

"Poor Stan," sighed Cath Fryer. "He's had a rough time of it in the past few years."

"Stan told us you and his late wife, Jeanie, were friends," said Gus.

"Jeanie was more of a mother to me," said Cath. "A lovely lady. I miss her."

"Stan mentioned his son, Stan, and the young lady who jilted him at the altar," said Gus.

"Tara Laing," said Cath. "I'm hardly likely to forget that day. We were outside the registry office, Dave, and me, waiting for them to come out. I've still got the box of confetti I bought to throw over them. It was the final straw for Jeanie. She lingered for a further eighteen months, perhaps two years, but the fight had gone. Young Stan went away soon after and only visited his father twice a year at most."

"Did you meet Tara?" asked Lydia.

"Oh, yes, dear," said Cath. "Quiet as a church mouse she was, gave no one a clue she would do something so cruel. I know it's not right to say, but if you stood on Stan's right-hand side, he was a handsome lad. Without the accident, he could have had his pick of the girls around town. Tara seemed happy enough whenever we saw the two of them together. But thirty minutes before she was supposed to walk into the registry office with her dad, the silly girl decided she couldn't go through with it."

"Did Tara marry and have children with someone else?" asked Gus.

"Not a bit, Mr Freeman. Tara's in her thirties now and recently retired from a career as an adult film actress. As if young Stan didn't have enough pain in his life. I pray he doesn't find her on the internet. She had the nerve to call herself Jeanie Jones. No, before you ask, I have watched none of her movies. A bloke Dave works with mentioned her to him a year or two back. He went to school with Tara Laing, remembered when she was with Stan Jones and that Dave had mentioned what happened on the wedding day."

Gus shared a glance with Lydia.

"Is there anything you want to ask Mrs Fryer, Lydia?"

"I think we've got what we came for, guv," said Lydia. "and more besides."

"I'm here in the afternoons if you ever want to chat again," said Cath.

"You've been most helpful," said Gus. He was eager to get moving. Once they were outside on the pavement, Lydia turned towards the car.

"One more call to make before we stop by your place, Lydia," said Gus. "Mrs Fryer said the chap at the window appeared to be trying to attract someone's attention."

Lydia followed Gus across the road. The first face to appear was Harry Simpkins.

"Is Matt Merchant around?" asked Gus.

"Here I am, Mr Freeman." Matt Merchant appeared from behind a Renault. "I hope this is a genuine visit. Anne Marie is at college this afternoon, we're short-handed, and customers are waiting."

"Oh, it's genuine," said Gus. "Do you recall the police mentioning an Afro-Caribbean gentleman outside the garage at four on the day Richard died?"

"Of course, but as we told you, if they were regular customers, they would use the side door."

"How many Afro-Caribbean men aged around thirty do you know, Mr Merchant?"

"Several, I suppose, why?"

"Give me a name,"

"Carlos Watson,"

"How do you know him?"

"He plays football for one team that plays at the Gerard Buxton Sports Arena,"

"Do you have his number?"

"It should be in the league handbook. I've never had cause to ring Carlos before. He doesn't bring his car here. What's going on?"

"Humour me," said Gus.

Five minutes later, a red-faced Matt Merchant returned.

"One mystery solved," said Gus. "Am I right?"

"I did not know it was Carlos," said Matt. "He told me just now that one of his teammates, Delroy West, usually drove him to football on Monday nights. Delroy's wife had started having contractions, and she wanted Delroy to get her to the hospital. The lads were driving past the garage on the way to Delroy's when Carlos remembered me mentioning I worked for Richard. Carlos hoped to grab a lift with me to football but couldn't make anyone hear. He hadn't visited the garage before, so he didn't realise he could have come to the side door. Delroy raced back to Walcot to collect his wife, and Carlos had to postpone the game that night because they couldn't get a team."

"What was it?" asked Lydia.

"Just a league game," said Matt.

"No, I meant the baby," said Lydia.

"I don't know. I never asked," said Matt.

"Well, that's another loose end tied off," said Gus. "By the way, I know you didn't know the man in the white van, but his name is Eddie Dolman. A painter and decorator who went to school with Richard. We've learned they hung around together as teenagers and as young men too."

"I knew he looked familiar," said Matt, "but I haven't seen him since that day."

"So, that bloke Dolman was here in the morning," said Harry Simpkins, who had stopped work to listen. "A youngster from London on a day trip, probably to offload drugs, was across the road in the early afternoon, and a West Indian footballer came here later in the day to see Matt. If it wasn't one of them who killed Richard, who was it then?"

"A fair question, Mr Simpkins," said Gus. "We'll let you know in due course."

"You've got someone in mind then, Mr Freeman," said Matt Merchant.

"Ever hopeful, Mr Marchant. Ever hopeful. Good day to you both."

Gus and Lydia crossed the street to the Focus, and Gus drove them out of Swindon to Wroughton and through the village of Avebury.

"Have you ever visited this village, Lydia?" he asked.

"We've driven past the stones many times," she replied. "But Alex and I have never stopped to walk around them. They're older than Stonehenge, aren't they?"

"There's evidence to suggest they're older, yes," said Gus. "The Neolithic monument contains three stone circles, one hundred stones in total around the village. Avebury henge is one of Britain's best-known prehistoric sites and contains the world's largest megalithic stone circle. History on your doorstep."

"Have you ever walked around the site, guv?" Lydia asked.

"What do you think?" he replied. "Always too busy to stop."

When they arrived at Alex and Lydia's house in Chippenham, Lydia invited Gus indoors to wait.

"You carry on, Lydia," said Gus. "I'll sit in the car and ponder the case. I do my best pondering in familiar spots such as this car and outside my garden shed at the allotments."

"I won't be long, I promise," she replied.

Fifteen minutes later, Lydia returned. A wide orange headband dragged her damp hair back off her face. The multi-coloured blouse and calf-length skirt had gone, replaced by an orange t-shirt and black leather skirt. A dress Gus had seen before. To say it was short was generous. Only someone with great legs could get away with it. Lydia didn't have a problem on that score.

"I hope you'll explain the change of clothing to Alex," said Gus.

"Don't worry, guv," said Lydia. "I'll tell him you were the perfect gentleman."

"I should hope so too, young lady," said Gus. "I have my reputation to protect."

Twenty-five minutes later, they were back in the Old Police Station car park.

"Do you have the killer in mind, guv?" asked Lydia as they waited for the lift.

"What three things do we need for murder, Lydia?" asked Gus.

"Means, motive, and opportunity, guv," she replied.

"Getting hold of a gun these days isn't the problem it once was. As for motive, I still don't understand who wanted Richard Chaloner dead and why. Nobody we've interviewed who was in Swindon on the day of the murder had either means or motive, even if they had the opportunity."

The lift arrived, and the pair rode to the first floor.

"That sounds as if we're still miles away, guv," said Lydia.

"We're close, Lydia," said Gus. "The missing pieces of the jigsaw are just out of reach."

Chapter Ten

"WELCOME BACK, YOU TWO," said Neil.

"Is everything okay, Lydia?" asked Blessing. "What prompted the change of clothes?"

"Trust a woman to notice," laughed Lydia. "Don't suppose you did, Neil?"

"As I'm a married man. Melody insists I'm not supposed to notice," said Neil.

"I noticed," said Alex. "I'm sure there's a simple explanation."

"Don't forget, I didn't see you, Lydia," said Luke. "I drove direct to Gablecross."

"Yes, Alex, a simple explanation. Ralph Robinson smokes forty a day despite the warnings," said Gus. "Lydia wanted to freshen up, so, after we left the garage, we returned here via Chippenham."

"I didn't realise you were revisiting the garage, guv," said Neil.

"Do you remember when there was a craze for filling a gymnasium with dominoes, Neil?" asked Gus. "Then a flick of the wrist set a quarter of a million tiles in motion. Well, today was like that. Stan Jones gave us a name. Eddie Dolman, white van man, painter and decorator, a pal of Richard Chaloner."

"That's only one tile, guv," said Blessing.

"Sometimes, that's all it takes," said Gus, tapping his nose.

"I've been with him every minute," shrugged Lydia. "Don't ask me what he's found."

"I spent my time wisely in the car while you were indoors, making yourself presentable," said Gus. "Although, as always, you stretched the limits of acceptable office wear."

"Sorry, guv," said Lydia. "My suit's at the dry cleaners."

"Right," said Gus. "Time is tight. Lydia and I will struggle to get our reports updated this afternoon. We made an unscheduled stop at the garage on top of the three appointments Luke had organised. So let's quickly debrief what we discovered, add it to the work you've been doing in our absence, and assess where we are."

"I received the information we requested from the Hub an hour ago, guv," said Alex. "You already called me with the news that Stan Jones identified Eddie Dolman. We've had time to check the Round Table, Folk Club, and CAMRA member details. Dolman is a folk music fan and a real ale drinker. Those were the activities he shared in common with Richard Chaloner."

"They attended primary and secondary schools in Pine-hurst," added Neil.

"Chaloner and Dolman lived less than a quarter of a mile from one another from birth until they were in their late twenties," said Blessing. "Dolman got married and moved into a house with his wife, Louise, in Penhill."

"We know Chaloner was single until he met Eve," said Gus. "Did he live with his parents until he married?"

"I'd need to check that, guv," said Luke. "I don't recall that information being in the murder file."

"Anything else that brought Dolman and Chaloner together?"

"They both attended the youth club in Pinehurst until they reached eighteen," said Neil. "Then I guess they started visiting pubs legally, which led to the love of a proper pint."

"Says the man who drinks lager," said Luke.

"I know we haven't included him before," said Gus, "but can you check for Jeff Hughes's name on the same lists as Chaloner and Dolman? I noticed the name in Neil and Blessing's reports of their conversation with Eve Chaloner."

"Got it, guv," said Alex. "Yes, he's a member of the Round Table branch and CAMRA. We can soon find out where he lived and went to school. If Richard Chaloner chose him as his best man, then they must have stayed close throughout their lives."

"Is Jeff Hughes married?" asked Blessing. "The wedding photographs at Eve Chaloner's house didn't show him with anyone. As for Eddie Dolman, he got married fifteen years earlier. That could have been when the trio started spending less time together. It would help explain the argument over the electrical fault. If Hughes had asked for a favour that morning, Chaloner might have relented. Hughes was still a close friend and not someone Chaloner bumped into at the odd real ale function. Louise Dolman might have had more claim on Eddie's free time than Richard Chaloner by then."

"Delicately put, Blessing," said Gus. "yes, petticoat government remained alive and well."

"I've confirmed the same school and the same youth club for Jeff Hughes, guv," said Alex.

"Luke, we need to interview those two," said Gus. "Don't accept excuses. Tell them to attend Gablecross Police Station at nine-thirty tomorrow morning. You know the drill if they disagree."

"Will do, guv," said Luke. "Who do you want with you?"

"I'll drive direct to Gablecross. Can you collect Blessing from Worton Farm, please? I'll see you both in Reception."

"What's next, guv?" asked Neil.

"Back to this morning's chat with Stan Jones. As I told Alex, Stan's eyesight is unreliable. He thought he saw a man and a woman that afternoon. Cath Fryer told us this afternoon that it was two men. When I asked Matt Merchant whether he knew anyone matching the new description, he realised that lads with dreadlocks played for another team at the sports arena in Wootton Bassett on Monday nights. Carlos Watson wanted a lift to football; it was a simple as that. Watson's pal had an emergency, and Carlos tried, but failed, to catch the attention of someone working inside."

"Nothing sinister then, guv," said Neil. "They could have avoided that mystery by asking the right people the right questions two years ago."

"It wouldn't have saved Richard Chaloner," said Gus. "Someone still wanted him dead. That's who we need to identify. The motive should become clearer once we've got that step out of the way."

"Did Ralph Robinson provide anything new, guv?" asked Luke.

"Not a jot, Luke," said Gus.

"Ralph and his wife, Betty, are as objectionable as one another," said Lydia. "She may suspect what lay behind his supposed twice-yearly visits to South Marston Cemetery, but they're still together."

"I imagine Luke told you the lurid details?" asked Gus.

"Yes, guv," said Blessing. "I wasn't a fan of Shakespeare at school. The language was dated and impossible to understand. I never imagined anyone using it to, you know...."

"There's an old saying, Blessing," said Gus. "There's nowt as strange as folk. I wouldn't worry unduly; Ms Kimble has retired now."

"We haven't exhausted the seamier side of life in Swindon though, Blessing," said Lydia. "Cath Fryer told us more about Stan Jones's son and the love of his life."

Gus gave the others the highlights of Stan's doomed relationship with Tara Laing and her subsequent lucrative career in front of the camera.

"Blimey, guv," said Neil. "Both Stan senior and Mrs Fryer described Tara as a quiet, timid girl. It's always the quiet ones that are the worst, isn't it?"

"Using Jeanie Jones as her stage name was rubbing salt in the wounds, guv," said Alex.

"Does this woman still live in Swindon, guv?" asked Blessing.

"Mrs Fryer didn't say, Blessing," said Gus. "I wonder how we could find out?"

"Tara Laing had no connection to Richard Chaloner or any of the others we've spoken to, did she?" asked Alex.

"You could ask Hughes and Dolman tomorrow whether they knew her," said Neil.

"If nobody but young Stan knew her, perhaps we can forget her, guv," said Lydia.

"It doesn't leave many people we can interrogate to unearth the killer, does it, guv?" asked Luke.

"Lydia and I will update the Freeman Files now," said

Gus, "while our memories are still fresh. The rest of you can carry on searching for missing links in that data that Divya slaved over. Luke needs to arrange tomorrow's interviews, and Blessing, you could try Cath Fryer to see whether she knows the whereabouts of Tara Laing."

"What about Stan Jones junior, guv?" asked Lydia. "His father never mentioned having a mobile number for him, did he?"

"No, I got the distinct impression young Stan cut his ties with the town after Tara left him at the altar. He returns to the house when his job brings him this way to collect official documents. He doesn't sound the type to receive personal mail if any. Did we start a search for him on social media?"

"He was never on our radar, guv," said Alex. "I'll add it to the list of things we can tackle when you're in Swindon in the morning."

"Stan and Cath told us it was only twice a year Stan turned up unannounced," said Lydia. "Stan senior thought it was Easter this year. He said his son enjoyed springtime. It makes sense he'd turn up in the next three months. Perhaps, if we can't find him another way, we should write to him at Stan's address. That way, we'd know he got the message. If we asked Stan to get his son to give us a ring, he might forget."

"How can he tell us anything about Richard Chaloner's murder?" asked Blessing. "He's only ever in town four days a year at most."

"Blessing's right, guv," said Neil. "There's nothing to say they knew one another in the brief time they spent on the same street. Stan worked a twelve-hour shift from six at night to six in the morning. I doubt if he got out of bed before two. Most blokes his age would make the most of those few hours of free time, not sit at home watching what was going on across the street."

"It won't hurt to check Stan out on social media," said Gus. "You can also ask his father if he has a number to call. Ask if he has any idea when he's due to drop in again this year."

"Would there be any post at the address for him now, guv?" asked Lydia.

"Possibly, Lydia," said Gus, "but it's more than my job's worth to interfere with the Royal Mail without a warrant."

"I've found details from the 1991 Census, guv," said Alex. "The Three Amigos shared a house in Pinehurst. The record suggests they moved there aged eighteen in 1990. Eddie Dolman got married in 2000. The 2001 Census shows only Chaloner and Hughes resident at the same address."

"Jeff Hughes still lives there, guv," said Neil. "He never married, but he has a partner, Lamai."

"Local girl?" asked Gus.

"Thailand, guv," said Neil. "Lamai is in her early twenties."

Blessing was just ending a phone call.

"What have you got, Blessing?" asked Gus.

"Mrs Fryer was able to tell me where Tara Laing lives, guv," said Blessing. "I had to ask her to spell it for me. Tara is living in splendid isolation on the island of Barra, in the Outer Hebrides. The nearest place with a name on the map is Buaile nam Bodach. I've tried to translate it from Gaelic, and the best I can come up with is the ghost's milking parlour. Don't hold me to that, though."

"A remote island," said Gus. "Tara wasn't taking any chances of her ex-boyfriend driving his truck through her front door, was she?"

"We'd only be guessing why Tara chose that island as her retirement home, guv," said Luke. "It's more likely she wanted to leave the world she worked in as far behind her as possible."

"You might be right, Luke," said Gus. "Let's call it a wrap for the day. But, sorry, I couldn't resist it. So Lydia and I will get on with those reports while you continue tracing links connecting Chaloner, Dolman, and Hughes."

At five o'clock, the office emptied. Gus was re-reading his notes on Matt Merchant. He wondered whether Suzie had plans for tonight. Gus checked his phone, but there was no message. He saved his updated files and closed his computer. Tomorrow was another day, and the meetings at Gablecross could prove illuminating.

As he passed the London Road HQ, he spotted Kenneth Truelove marching across the visitor's car park, heading for his new limousine. Very nice too, thought Gus. Why not accept one of the job's perks, especially if you knew the fun would stop in around eighteen months.

Gus sped up as he left the town's outskirts. No way was he letting the Chief Constable glide past him. But, he needn't have worried. The traffic lights changed as Gus passed, and by the time Kenneth moved forward again, Gus was on the Lydeway, indicating to turn right towards Urchfont.

Old habits are hard to break, and Gus slowed as he approached the allotments. He hadn't seen Bert Penman in the flesh for days. When your friends are in their mid-eighties, it's not sensible to leave long gaps between seeking them out. One day it might be too late, and Gus didn't want to hear Bert had gone to the great allotment in the sky without saying goodbye.

The church clock was gathering itself to chime the half-hour. Suzie could hold the fort until he got home. Bert was busy on his plot of land, hunting for elusive blackcurrants. Irene North would have received the best crop in early August, but Bert's variety consistently outperformed everyone else's. His basket was over half full.

"Good of you to drop by, Mr Freeman," said Bert without looking up from his labours.

"We keep missing one another, Bert," said Gus.

"Who said I missed you," said Bert.

"Has Clemency Bentham been here this afternoon, keeping you company?"

"The Reverend worked on her patch for an hour, Mr Freeman," said Bert. "She's listening to my words of wisdom. I'm impressed at what she's able to produce, considering the state of the soil Frank North left her."

"Only an hour?" asked Gus. "Did she have sick parishioners to visit?"

"That will be this evening now, I reckon. But, no, the suffering Bishop wanted to speak to her."

"You mean the suffragan Bishop, Bert," said Gus. "They report to the Bishop of the diocese."

"I bow to your superior knowledge, Mr Freeman,"

"Even though I'm no fan of religion, Bert, I've picked up some knowledge over the years. Hard not to when you're a young copper on streets in the shadow of Salisbury Cathedral spire."

"Did you have another reason for stopping by on your way home, Mr Freeman?" asked Bert.

"I told you. I hadn't seen you for a while, nothing more."

"A tough case," said Bert. "That will be it. I've learned to recognise the signs. When I've taken these blackcurrants home for Irene, no doubt you'll return here and fetch that seat of yours from the shed. You'll need a light sweater this evening if you intend to sit and ponder. You don't want a chill in the kidneys at your age. The breeze can have a bite to it on a September evening."

"I'll have to see what Suzie has planned, Bert," said Gus. "An ex-colleague is in the hospital in Swindon. Suzie visited her yesterday evening. I want to consider various elements of the case we're dealing with this week, but the picture I see is constantly moving in and out of focus."

"I get days like that," said Bert. "I tried to tell Irene we needed a new TV. Instead, she rapped my knuckles and suggested I cut back on the cider."

"Any regrets about you and Irene living under the same roof, Bert?" asked Gus.

"Not so far, Mr Freeman," said Bert. "The neighbours have stopped giving us sideways glances. Irene reckons they think she's my carer. I reminded Irene that I could look after myself, thank you very much."

"I can see Irene's logic," said Gus. "The villagers can accept her moving in with you to look after you and relax. Now, they'll stop spreading rumours you're at it like knives every night."

Bert shook his head.

"People have nothing better to do than think dirty thoughts, Mr Freeman. The Reverend worried that was why the Bishop's subordinate wanted to see her. If they've stopped gossiping about Irene and me, they've moved on to my grandson and his lady friend."

"It could be a simple matter regarding the church behind us, Bert," said Gus.

"I hope they aren't considering ripping out the pews and replacing them with modern seating," said Bert. "Those pews have been there for a century and more. Pews are uncomfortable by design. I don't hold with the happy-clappy business they go for today."

"You're a fine one to criticise, Bert Penman. You didn't step inside the doors of that place for decades. Clemency tried to persuade you to rejoin her flock when she arrived in the village, without luck."

"Irene thought we should put in an appearance," said Bert, "to keep Brett company. Although, for the past couple of Sundays, he's been over Beckhampton way tending to racehorses. I didn't intend making a habit of attending morning service, anyway."

"I can understand that, Bert," said Gus. Time to get to the bungalow to speak with Suzie.

As he got in the driver's seat, he called out to Bert.

"If it became a habit, Irene might get ideas."

"It won't take you long to solve that case of yours, Mr Freeman. You joined the dots there quick enough."

Bert gave Gus a friendly wave and turned back to finish his harvesting.

Suzie was in the kitchen when Gus entered the hallway of the bungalow.

"Did your interviews last longer than expected?" she asked.

"No, I spotted Bert at the allotments and stopped for a chat. What's the latest?"

"Vicky continues to make progress," said Suzie. "I'll visit her tomorrow evening if that's okay?"

"Of course," said Gus. "That wonderful smell from the kitchen tells me we're eating in tonight. How long have I got?"

"Half an hour," said Suzie.

"I need to shower and change after spending the day in Swindon. We've got several characters we can eliminate from our enquiries, but no matter what we've done so far, we can't find a motive for the murder."

"You thought it was personal," said Suzie.

"I know it was," said Gus. "Everything I've ever learned as a copper screams to me that someone wanted Richard Chaloner to suffer. They tried to hide the truth by making it appear to be a robbery, but it didn't fool me."

"Have your shower," said Suzie. "We'll eat dinner, and then you can take me through the case step-by-step."

"Another quiet night in? The neighbours will talk."

"They'll have plenty to gossip over next week," said Suzie.

Thursday, 6 September 2018

"I'LL SEE you at around half-past seven," said Suzie as she stood by her Golf at eight-fifteen.

"Okay," said Gus. "I don't expect to be home late this evening. So we'll eat at the Fox and Hounds tonight for a change. I'll give them a ring later."

"No visit to the allotments tonight."

"September evenings can get chilly, I hear," said Gus. "The weekend is almost upon us."

"Good luck today," said Suzie. "Why did you ask Luke to bring Blessing this morning?"

"I need Blessing to ride shotgun when I interview Eddie Dolman," said Gus. "That keeps the Chief Constable off my case. Luke can handle Jeff Hughes alone. Luke's feeling left out of things at present, which isn't my intention. I'm desperate to keep him with the team. There aren't many opportunities to give someone added responsibility without putting another person's nose out of joint."

"I'm sure you'll keep him sweet," said Suzie. "See you tonight."

Gus followed the VW Golf as far as the junction and flashed his lights as Suzie turned left towards Devizes. He turned right and took the quieter scenic route to Upavon and followed the A346 through Marlborough to Gablecross. He congratulated himself on his timing when he pulled up beside Luke's car in the car park at two minutes to nine.

Luke and Blessing were still negotiating Reception when Gus joined them. The duty sergeant rescued the three of them from an over-zealous youngster who looked as if he was in the building for work experience. The sergeant insisted he was nineteen, but Gus had his doubts.

"We've had to limit you to Interview Room Three this morning," said the sergeant. "Tom Spencer needs more space."

"Tom found the tractor thieves," said Luke. "He said he would."

"He certainly did," said the sergeant. "We've got five men in the cells waiting for an interview, and a convoy of stolen vehicles are getting returned to their owners as we speak."

"Let's hope we can add to the feel-good vibe around the station," said Gus.

Gus, Luke, and Blessing settled themselves in the interview room. Luke and Blessing got things ready for half-past nine.

"Do we see Dolman and Hughes together, guv?" asked Blessing. "I'm surplus to requirements, aren't I?"

"No, we'll see them separately, Blessing," said Gus. "Hughes will have to wait in Reception until we've finished with his former housemate. Then, you and I will handle Dolman. After that, Luke can see Hughes alone. Luke can observe from behind the one-way glass for the first session, and then we'll swap places."

Gus took his team through the pattern of questions he hoped to follow.

"We can't be too regimented in our approach," he reminded them. "If you spot a potential opening, pursue it as vigorously as you can. Something has to give, sooner or later."

At nine-thirty, on the dot, the duty sergeant returned to the interview room with Eddie Dolman. The painter and decorator had discarded his overalls and wore casual clothes —a maroon sweater over a magnolia shirt and faded blue jeans. Gus corrected himself. The shirt was cream coloured.

"Take a seat, Mr Dolman," said Gus. "Freeman's the name, a consultant with Wiltshire Police. Detective Constable Umeh is also present. Did you decide against bringing legal representation with you this morning?"

"Nobody mentioned I needed a solicitor," said Eddie.

Gus wanted him on the back foot from the outset. He was convinced Eddie Dolman held one of the missing pieces to this case.

"Our colleague, Detective Sergeant Sherman, told you why we wanted to speak with you this morning. We're taking a fresh look at the murder of your friend, Richard Chaloner, two years ago."

"We had been friends since we were kids, but that changed over the last few years."

"Remind us how you met," asked Gus.

"In the playground when we were five," said Eddie.

"At school in Pinehurst,"

"That's right. We were always in the same class until we

went to secondary school. Richard was brighter than Jeff and me."

"Jeff Hughes?"

"Jeff drove me here this morning. He called last night and asked if I needed a lift. The first time we'd spoken for several years."

"You went around together outside of school too, didn't you? We understand you attended the same youth club."

"That's right," said Eddie. "We stuck together despite everything."

"Who suggested sharing the same house?" asked Gus.

"Richard, I think. It's a long time ago now. We got on, and it worked out cheaper between the three of us."

"So, from the age of eighteen to twenty-eight, you shared a home with Richard Chaloner and Jeff Hughes?"

"We had some great times," said Eddie. "Three young lads, footloose and fancy-free. We were working daytime jobs, earning decent money, and enjoying life evenings and weekends."

"Did you meet many girls?" asked Blessing.

"Of course we did, but that wasn't important in the first few years. We made friends with people from other parts of Swindon. Most were lads, but some were girls. The three of us had a girlfriend from time to time, nothing serious."

"Then you met Louise," said Gus.

"Jeff Hughes saw Louise first and went out with her for a month. I stole Louise from him. We got married later that same year. Jeff and Richard didn't speak to me for a while after that. Richard thought I'd let the side down. He and Jeff had belonged to the Round Table branch ever since they were old enough, but that fun and friendship stuff made me suspicious. Jeff told me on the way here that because the upper age limit was forty-five, he had to leave a year ago."

"We understand you kept in touch with Richard and Jeff at CAMRA and the Folk Club. Did that stop when you married Louise?"

"I couldn't afford to go as often as before," said Eddie. "We've got two kids, a boy and a girl. So it wasn't always practical to get to Highworth or Wroughton for a night out."

"So, it strained relations between the three of you after you got married," said Gus.

"For a while. Richard was mad at me because I left at short notice, and they found it tough holding onto the house."

"They could have advertised for someone to share the load," said Gus.

"You don't understand. That wasn't possible, under the circumstances. Anyway, as it happened, we needn't have got married in a rush. It was a false alarm. A couple of years later, Louise was pregnant for real, and Jeff and I started talking again. I did some work at his parent's house in Pinehurst. As I was finishing for the day, he turned up and asked if I fancied going for a drink one night. That set things right between us."

"Did you ever heal the rift with Richard?" asked Blessing.

"We did, and we didn't," said Eddie. "It was never the same as when we were teenagers—all for one, and one for all. We were civil to one another when we met. Let's put it that way."

"It's taken a long time to identify you as the man seen on the forecourt of Richard's garage on the morning of the day he died. Although you and Richard weren't the bosom buddies you had been as kids, it must have shocked you to learn of his death. Why didn't you come forward at the time?"

"I didn't want to get involved," said Eddie.

"Why, I wonder?" said Gus.

"I didn't kill Richard," said Eddie. "We argued that morning because he was bloody-minded as usual. I wanted a quick check of my electrical fault. But, he had to stick to his principles and look after his loyal customers first. After all the years, Jeff and I stayed loyal to him. I knew the police would latch onto the argument and then add that to us falling out over Louise and the money. I would have been their prime suspect if the police didn't have anyone else in the frame. So I kept my mouth shut, and when nobody from Gablecross went near Jeff Hughes, I realised he'd adopted the same approach."

"Did you get an invitation to Richard and Eve's wedding?" asked Blessing.

"No, the first I knew of it was when the wedding photos appeared in the Advertiser."

"Did it surprise you to see Richard get married?"

"He wasn't gay. Richard just wasn't worried whether or not he met the right girl in the old days. If it happened, it happened."

"Jeff Hughes was the same, I imagine?" asked Gus.

Eddie laughed.

"Louise said Jeff didn't see her as an equal. That was why she threw her lot in with me. Look at him now, shacked up with a mail-order bride, twenty years his junior. On the way here this morning, Jeff admitted he was already regretting it."

"What do you know about Tara Laing?" asked Gus.

"What does she have to do with Richard's murder?" asked Eddie.

"Ever since we started looking at this case, I've struggled to find anyone with a motive to kill Richard."

"I can't imagine Richard ever knew her to speak to," said Eddie. "Jeff Hughes wouldn't have either. We saw her in Swindon when we were in our early twenties, but Tara was way too young to mix with us."

"Did you ever see her with a boyfriend?" asked Gus.

"It didn't register if we did," said Eddie. "As I said, the places we went to were popular with older people. We rarely went anywhere to mix with people younger than ourselves after we left the youth club."

"Do you recall when Tara Laing and Stan Jones were due to get married?" asked Gus.

"That was big news for a few days when it happened," said Eddie. "Getting cold feet and leaving the groom standing like a lemon. Well, it doesn't happen every day, does it?"

"Fifteen years ago now," said Gus.

"Not quite," said Eddie. "It was the end of the first week in November."

"How can you be so definite?" asked Blessing.

"The couple had booked the wedding for Saturday afternoon. Louise went into labour at three o'clock. Our son, Tyson, was born at seven on Sunday morning. The nurses were discussing what happened at the registry office throughout the night."

Gus had to admit Eddie Dolman didn't have a motive to kill Richard Chaloner. He was desperate to find the connection they were missing, but it still eluded him. When Luke had spoken to Jeff Hughes, Gus wanted to go through both men's replies, searching for discrepancies, anything that hinted they were hiding something. Was the picture becoming sharper, or was the fog descending altogether?

Chapter Eleven

"WHAT HAPPENS NOW?" asked Eddie.

"I'll call the desk sergeant," said Gus. "He'll escort Jeff Hughes here, and you can wait in Reception. After that, we may need to speak with you again."

Two minutes later, Luke entered the room with the desk sergeant and Jeff Hughes.

Eddie Dolman glanced at his friend, nodded, and followed the sergeant from the room.

"Eddie will wait for you in Reception," explained Gus. "DS Sherman will be in charge of this interview. My colleague and I will leave you now.

Gus and Blessing went into the corridor and found their way to the viewing room.

While Luke went through the usual preamble, Blessing asked Gus:

"What did you make of Eddie Dolman, guv?"

"Eddie told us something, but I can't work out what it meant."

Blessing sat in a chair and watched Luke get to work.

"Why did you give Eddie a lift here this morning?" asked Luke.

"How did you hear that?" asked Jeff.

"I'm a detective," said Luke. "You two go way back, don't you?"

"Ever since we were kids at school. It's not a crime."

"Two's company," said Luke.

"What's that supposed to mean?"

"Was there something that kept the three of you together through your teens and into your twenties?"

"We were mates," said Jeff.

"You never fell out?" asked Luke.

"We were okay until Louise came on the scene."

"Richard was a gregarious individual, according to everyone the police spoke to two years ago. Richard had girlfriends, but nobody serious. Did he fancy Louise?"

"Richard was looking for the right girl. I never asked whether he thought Louise was the one. I went with Louise for a while, but things didn't work out, and the next thing I know, Eddie's with her. Louise and Eddie got married, and suddenly we were one short when the mortgage payment became due. Richard wasn't happy."

"Eddie made a life without you," said Luke. "Two children, his painting and decorating business. You saw less of him at the Folk Club and the CAMRA meetings."

"People move on, don't they? So we muddled along, just the two of us, making our way in business—Richard with his garage, me with my window cleaning firm. Then, one night, I was with Richard in town, and while I was getting the drinks, I noticed him chatting with a woman. It wasn't unusual. He could chat to anybody, but I'd never seen Richard so animated or engaged. When I gave him his drink, he told me he'd found the girl he would marry. It was as simple as that. Richard asked me to be his best man within weeks. Eve would have been the making of him. They were made for each other."

"Why didn't you come forward when Richard died?"

"Don't know what you mean. I visited Eve as soon as she returned from Greece. I told her how sorry I was for her loss. She said I must miss him too, which I did. When the police finally released the body, I helped Eve with the funeral arrangements."

"The police never contacted you?" asked Luke.

"They had no cause to," said Jeff.

"Did you know Eddie argued with Richard that morning?"

"Of course I didn't, not at the time. I do now because Eddie mentioned it in the car as we drove here."

"Where were you on the day Stan Jones and Tara Laing were due to get married?"

"Heaven only knows," said Jeff.

"Did you know Tara Laing?"

Jeff shook his head.

"For the tape, Mr Hughes," said Luke.

"She was a child the last time I saw her. We were much older than Tara. I didn't know her."

"What about Stan Jones? The young man Tara couldn't bring herself to marry. Had you met him?"

"He was the same age as Tara. So why should we know him?"

"Did you spot that, Blessing?" asked Gus as they watched from the other room.

"Twice, guv," said Blessing.

"Time for us to join in the fun. Three against one isn't fair odds, is it? Never mind."

Gus didn't knock. He and Blessing entered Interview Room Three.

"Gus Freeman and DC Blessing Umeh have entered the room," said Luke.

"Eddie Dolman gave us the first hint of the truth earlier, Mr Hughes. We know what happened. There's no point denying it any longer. Eddie said the three of you stuck together despite everything. It was necessary to stay close, wasn't it? Two's company, and three's a crowd. I asked Eddie why you and Richard didn't advertise for another housemate when he got married. It wasn't possible, under the circumstances, was his response to that. Then when he visited the garage on the day Richard died to ask for a favour, Richard refused. What did Eddie say about that? He said that after the years Eddie had stayed loyal to Richard, he couldn't do that one small thing for him. DS Sherman watched that interview and picked up the clues. When he asked where you were on the day Stan Jones and Tara Laing were due to get married, you almost jumped out of your chair. You hid it well and recovered, but when asked if you had met Stan Jones, there it was again."

"Stan Jones is our missing link," said Luke. "Stan Jones junior, the lad who picked up a discarded firework thinking it had didn't ignite."

"Two's company, three's a gang, perhaps," said Gus. "Who was the ringleader?"

"Richard," said Jeff Hughes, his shoulders slumped.

"That flies in the face of everything we've heard," said Gus.

"Richard tried to make recompense for that night for the rest of his life. He sponsored various events for children's charities, the air ambulance, you name it. We went out on November the fifth that year, not intent on making trouble, but we were just stupid. We cycled around the streets, throwing lit fireworks at front doors, dropping them in litter bins. When we cycled along Ponting Street, one banger didn't ignite, and a young boy was waiting in the doorway, watching the rockets in the sky. His parents were indoors. As we raced away to the next street, the lad must have bent to pick up the firework. I heard the bang and his screams. We cycled faster. Nobody linked the incident with us, and as long as we stuck together and never mentioned it again, Richard thought we were safe."

"Bicycles," said Blessing. "Was that how you got around in those days?"

"I couldn't afford a car, and nor could the others," said Jeff. "I hadn't long left school. It was November the fifth, 1989. Stan must have been seven, maybe eight years old. There were reports in the paper about the accident. Then, after two weeks, the dust settled, and the world moved on."

"Not for Stan Jones," said Gus.

"An accident such as Stan's wasn't a rare occurrence years ago," said Jeff. "The campaign for tighter controls over the sale of fireworks gained ground with each November casualty, but the momentum faded in the New Year. It was the anniversary of that night that forever brought the horror of what we'd caused home to us three."

"Richard persuaded you to stick together," said Luke. "Was it him who threw the banger?"

Jeff Hughes nodded.

"We cycled the two miles home to Pinehurst, throwing the rest of our fireworks over hedges and walls as we went. Then, a week later, Richard started talking about moving out of our homes to share a house. He wanted to make certain nobody broke ranks."

"You didn't break ranks for over ten years until Louise

came on the scene," said Gus. "That was the real reason for Richard shunning Eddie when he asked for help. Everyone believed Richard didn't marry until he met Eve because he was waiting for the right girl. The truth is, he expected you and Eddie to stay single. If you separated for any length of time, there was always the risk one of you would let something slip regarding your involvement in young Stan Jones's accident."

"Were you that much under his spell?" asked Luke.

"Richard could be very persuasive," said Jeff. "He was unhappy when I started seeing Louise. Richard told me she wasn't right for me, that I was better off as a bachelor. Perhaps that was why Louise and I drifted apart. Then, Eddie stepped into my shoes, and it was soon clear he wasn't prepared to listen to Richard anymore. Eddie and Louise married in 2000, and somehow Richard and I found the money to keep that roof over our heads. After that, it was touch and go."

"How were things between you and Richard?" asked Gus.

"We were both growing our respective businesses over the next five or six years. Although we shared the house, we had less spare time with each successive year. We still attended branch meetings at Round Table, visited the Folk Club in Highworth, and supported the Campaign for Real Ale functions. Our social life wasn't every night of the week as it had been in our teenage years. Eddie and Louise came to the Folk Club now and then, and they looked so happy. When Louise gave birth to Tyson, Eddie was like a dog with two tails. I didn't want to miss out on what they had, but I was in my early thirties, and most of the girls we met were married already, engaged, or not interested. Richard soon noticed I was searching online for a bride. We argued. I told him we'd shielded one another long enough. Nobody cared what happened so many years ago. Stan Jones had got on with his life, despite his scars. His girlfriend had changed her mind at the last minute, but Stan didn't live in Swindon any longer. So, how were we to know he wasn't married with children in another part of the country? His father lived across the road from Richard's garage. I asked Richard if any of the neighbours knew where Stan lived. Richard told me that according to people on Ponting Street, young Stan drove across Europe, driving his own truck, and had made a success of his life. Then we learned Eddie's son, Tyson had a sister, Rhiannon, and I redoubled my efforts to find a partner. I got several replies from my search, but for one reason or another, they fell through. I started writing to Lamai four years ago. When Richard and I were in town for a drink on the night he met Eve; I'd recently received a letter from Lamai. Richard knew I was keen on her, and he could tell from my reaction when I read her letter Lamai was just as interested."

"So, Richard decided if Lamai arrived from Thailand shortly, he had to alter his plans," said Gus. "Our impression was Richard and Eve were a match made in heaven. You're suggesting something quite different."

"Oh, Richard's reaction, when they met that night, was genuine," said Jeff. "We'd lived together for too long for him to fool me. It was just that Richard opened up to the possibility of something happening instead of repressing any feelings he had for a girl. I still had reservations over Lamai because of her age at that stage. When Richard met Eve, Lamai was several months away from her nineteenth birthday. I was still deciding if it was the right thing to do when Richard announced he and Eve were getting married. He asked me to be his best man. You know what happened next; they married in the Spring, and Richard died six months later."

"On Monday the seventh of November," said Gus. "Yes, there's a pattern emerging, isn't there?"

"What happens now?" asked Jeff Hughes.

"We pass the results of our case reviews further up the chain of command," said Gus. "It's for others to decide what action to take for an incident that occurred thirty years ago. We'll call the desk sergeant to collect you, Mr Hughes. You can drive Mr Dolman home. I don't mind if you tell him your secret's out at last."

Jeff Hughes stood and waited while Luke made the call.

"We were idiots to go along with what Richard decided," he said. "He tried to salve his conscience with his charity work, but it will come out now. Did you know that Matt Merchant would have ended up in jail the way he was going? Instead, Richard gave him a job and helped keep him on the straight and narrow."

The desk sergeant tapped on the door. Jeff Hughes left the room.

"He didn't ask, guv," said Blessing.

"I know," said Gus. "We need to work fast. It's September already. If they are in danger, we'll need to arrange protection for them with Geoff Mercer."

"Amazing, isn't it?" said Luke. "They built such a strong wall around themselves after that night, yet it crumbled in minutes."

"You followed my instructions to the letter, Luke," said Gus. "I asked you both to listen for a possible lead, and you used what Eddie Dolman said to prise open Jeff Hughes's defence. Blessing and I came to join you and pursued that lead with vigour. Hughes didn't have an answer. Well done."

"Thanks, guv," said Luke. "You threw me for a second though when you mentioned the bicycles, Blessing."

"It was obvious, wasn't it?" she replied. "Gus always used that bicycle as the reason to dismiss the attack as a robbery. He also thought it ruled out a connection to a criminal gang. It had to be important, but we could never fathom why. As soon as Hughes told us they rode everywhere on bicycles as teenagers, that was it. Matt Merchant said Richard cycled to work every day from Pinehurst and continued to cycle after he married. Richard didn't own a modern bicycle. It was the old-fashioned variety, with a comfortable saddle and panniers. It might not have been the same one he rode that night in November 1989, but I bet it was the same model."

"Stan Jones could have seen Richard's bicycle beside the garage when he lived with his father," said Luke. "He recognised it."

"You wouldn't forget it, would you, Luke?" said Blessing.

"But young Stan wasn't there that night two years ago," said Luke.

"His rig wasn't there," said Blessing. "We know he parked it on the outskirts of town when visiting his father. But that doesn't mean he wasn't in Swindon."

"We have work to do," said Gus. "Time to vacate this interview room and return to the office. Come on."

Blessing had to run to keep up with Gus as he strode along the passageways back to Reception. Luke was keeping pace with Gus until Tom Spencer appeared ahead of them.

"You can travel back in Gus's car, Blessing," he said. "I'll catch you up on the road."

"Have you had a good morning, Luke?" asked Tom.

"We've had a significant break in the case," said Luke.

"We aren't at the same stage as you, grilling the guilty parties, but we're much further forward than we were when we arrived."

"I'm glad," said Tom. "I'm too busy to hear it now, Luke. Perhaps you can tell me over that drink I mentioned yesterday?"

"I'd like that," said Luke.

When Luke turned into the Old Police Station car park, it was fast approaching noon. Gus and Blessing had already got out of the Focus and were walking to the lift.

"Wait for me," he called.

Luke parked his car and dashed across to get into the lift with Gus and Blessing.

"Sorry, I wanted to congratulate Tom Spencer on a job well done. He was curious how his old case was progressing. I told him as much as I thought sensible."

"Quite right, too," said Gus. "We're a long way from putting anyone in the frame for murder. Instead, we've uncovered a dark secret. Whether it was the catalyst for murder, we can't say for sure."

Alex, Neil, and Lydia were engrossed in their work when the others exited the lift.

"I hope you guys had a good morning," said Neil. "It's been heavy going for us, I'm afraid."

"What was the problem, Neil," asked Gus.

"Coffee, guv?" asked Blessing. Gus nodded. Luke followed Blessing to the restroom.

"We searched high and low on social media for signs of Stan Jones, guv. There's not a trace of him anywhere."

"We hoped to find a picture of his rig," said Lydia. "If Stan earned enough to buy his own vehicle, he must have been proud of it."

"Nothing," said Alex. "We switched our attention to the

membership listings for the three organisations. We hunted for more common links that might add to our list of persons of interest."

"Zilch," said Lydia. "There was nobody on the lists with any connection to a name we've uncovered during this investigation."

Blessing and Luke returned with coffees for everyone.

"As it's only just gone noon, we thought you wouldn't have stopped for lunch yet," she said. "We didn't get offered drinks at Gablecross."

Blessing glanced at Luke. One of us did, but Luke had told her that in confidence. In turn, Blessing told Luke about her successful dinner date last night with Jamie BT. Things were on an improving trend for both of them, it appeared.

"Right," said Gus. "We listened to Dolman and Hughes give us the agreed version of what happened in the years leading up to Chaloner's murder. Then Luke opened a tiny crack, and the dam burst. Hughes confessed that as teenagers, they had ridden through the streets of Swindon creating havoc by throwing fireworks with the inevitable results."

"They caused Stan Jones's disfigurement," said Lydia. "That's unbelievable."

"How come they didn't get caught, guv?" asked Neil.

"They cycled away before Stan's parents came outside," said Luke. "The street was empty, and Stan didn't know who threw the firework that exploded in his face. He might have told his parents there were three boys on bicycles, but at his age, he wouldn't know any of their names or that they lived just two miles away in Pinehurst."

"Hughes told us Chaloner threw the firework that did the damage," said Gus. "He was the ringleader and swore the others to secrecy. For years, they lived together, socialized together, and Chaloner kept them under his watchful eye."

"He wasn't the saint everyone thought he was," said Lydia.

"Chaloner tried to make amends with charity work and by giving others a helping hand," said Luke. "The murder file hinted Matt Merchant had his brushes with the law as a teenager. Hughes told us Chaloner gave Matt a job in a last-ditch attempt to keep him out of prison."

"It worked," said Neil. "He runs the business now."

"I feel sorry for Eve Chaloner," said Lydia. "When we complete our reports, she'll learn the truth about her late husband."

"At least Stan Jones will know who harmed his son," said Neil. "Hang on, do you think the son killed Richard Chaloner, guv?"

"I don't think there's any doubt young Stan had motive, Neil," said Gus. "It's means and opportunity we need to prove."

"How do we do that, guv," asked Alex.

"I want to track his movements from November 2004 to the present day," said Gus. "That's probably an impossible task, but let me explain my reasoning."

Gus stood up, walked to the nearest whiteboard, and added two dates:

November 5th, 1989

November 8th, 2003

Gus left a sizeable gap before writing:

November 7th, 2016

"Our story began on Bonfire Night in 1989 when Chaloner threw that firework with no regard for the damage it might cause. He didn't mean for anyone to get hurt, but

Stan Jones was too young to know what might happen. The blast scarred his left hand and face. Fourteen years later, after going out together for two years, Stan's girlfriend doesn't arrive for their registry office wedding."

"Then, thirteen years later, around the same time, someone shoots Richard Chaloner in his garage," said Alex. "Stan Jones is common to both the earlier dates, guv, but even if Jones was in the country on the day of the murder, why then?

"Why the gap, guv?" asked Neil.

"Do you mean, why did Jones wait twenty-seven years for his revenge over the firework incident? Or why did Jones shoot Chaloner thirteen years after Tara Laing walked out on him? Perhaps you meant why leave a sizeable gap between the dates."

"Is this where you get all Hercules Poirot, guv?" asked Lydia.

"I can thank my little grey cells, Lydia," said Gus. "The Chief Constable told me I was guilty of jumping in too soon when I first heard the details of this case. The first thing that struck me was the lack of panic after the killer shot Chaloner. I could see he'd done his homework on Matt Merchant and Harry Simpkins. I didn't understand the significance of the slashed bicycle tyre, but my grey cells warned me it was important. It was that which convinced me the robbery was an afterthought. The killer waited in the dark in the centre of the workshop after everyone had left. Chaloner left the office to investigate. The killer was someone he knew. It might have explained why there was no struggle. Chaloner accepted his fate."

"What was significant about the slashed tyre, guv?" asked Neil.

"It's the bike you need to concentrate on, Neil," said

Blessing. "I think it possible it was the same one Chaloner rode the night Stan Jones got hurt."

"Blimey," said Neil. "That could be tough to prove."

"Why?" asked Blessing. "The forensic team took the bike into evidence at Gablecross. They would have recorded every detail concerning that bike as it was part of a murder case. When they'd done with it, they would have returned it to Eve Chaloner at Shrivenham Road. Would Eve have thrown her husband's prized possession out already? I doubt it. We could check it out, get the model verified, and link it to the 1989 incident."

"That's one of several pieces to fit into our jigsaw, Blessing," said Gus. "We also need to place Stan Jones in the garage on Monday, the seventh of November, two years ago. But, unfortunately, I fear that might not be the last piece, and our team won't be capable of finding the pieces of the bigger picture."

"The big gap, guv," said Alex.

"The last thing I said to Kenneth Truelove and Geoff Mercer on Monday lunchtime was that I didn't believe Chaloner was our killer's first victim."

"It was the wedding that never was that was the trigger," said Luke.

"There could be female victims Jones targeted," said Lydia.

Gus shook his head.

"It's each of the above," he said. "November has been a significant month in Stan Jones's life. First, it was when he received the burns that caused him so much pain. Those scars resulted in him having a miserable childhood. Then, just when he thought he'd found happiness with Tara, she jilted him in November. His mother, Jeanie, had suffered from cancer for a while but battled to stay alive for her only son's wedding. Stan's father told us she gave up after that setback. I've checked the date she died. It was November the first, 2005."

Gus added the date to the list on the whiteboard.

"Was Lydia right to mention female victims, guv?" asked Neil.

"I fear so," said Gus.

"How do we find out?" asked Alex.

"Give Divya a photograph of Tara Laing, head and shoulders only, and ask her to find unsolved murders of women resembling Tara, in November, between 2005 and 2015."

"In the UK and mainland Europe, guv?" asked Alex.

"That's the size of it," said Gus.

"We're taking a punt with this, aren't we, guv?" asked Neil. "If Jones worked out Chaloner was responsible for his injuries, why didn't he attack him sooner? Why didn't he attack Tara Laing, anyway? She was the one who jilted him."

"Long-distance lorry driving must be a lonely existence, Neil," said Lydia. "Nothing to think about, except watching the road ahead for mile after mile and sleeping in your cab. With what happened in his childhood and then his experience with Tara, Stan must have spent thousands of hours going over how much he'd suffered. As Gus pointed out, November would be a trigger for dark thoughts every year. Remember what his father told us. Stan loves the springtime. It's the period of the year furthest from his traumas. When November comes around, he remembers Tara and how she crushed his hopes of marriage and children. If he saw a young girl who reminded him of Tara, he could act on those thoughts of revenge he'd harboured during the past months. He would be attacking a stranger, but in his twisted mind, he would be killing Tara Laing."

"That makes a kind of sense," said Neil, "but you haven't explained why he waited so long to kill Richard Chaloner."

"That's easy, Neil," said Blessing. "Stan's father told us his son came to visit him at Easter time this year. He also suggested young Stan kept in touch with local news while he was driving. Young Stan knew his mother had died, even though his father didn't have a number to call him. So, he could have seen a report of Richard and Eve's wedding in the spring, either on his travels or when he visited his father to collect his post. Can you imagine his reaction? Richard had never married. Then, suddenly, there he was, smiling at the camera with a beautiful woman by his side. No way was young Stan going to let the man responsible for the scars on his face have the life he'd dreamed of with Tara Laing. If Stan couldn't be happy, nor could Richard Chaloner."

"Well done, Blessing," said Gus. "We can't do any more until we get results from the Hub. Get your digital files updated, and I'll contact London Road. I imagine I'll need to hand over the files to the Chief Constable sooner rather than later. It will depend on how quickly Divya comes back with answers."

Chapter Twelve

AT THE END of another busy day, Gus drove home to the bungalow. He knew he was returning to an empty house. Suzie was halfway to the Great Western Hospital to visit Vicky Bennison. Unfortunately, he had nobody with whom to share his news.

As he stepped inside the bungalow, Gus heard the tinkle of a bicycle bell. Odd, how comforting that sound could be. It brought back memories of childhood when life was simpler and carefree. But, for Stan Jones, the sight of bicycles racing past his front door held darker, violent memories.

"Good afternoon, Gus," said Clemency. "I was on my way back to the Rectory when I spotted your car. Is Suzie not home yet?"

"Suzie's visiting her colleague in the hospital again," said Gus. "She'll be home by seven-thirty. Did you want to speak to her?"

"Nothing that can't wait until the weekend," said Clemency. She was already turning her bicycle around, preparing to cycle out of the driveway. "I wanted to tell her one of my parishioners was getting things together for a jumble sale. I spotted several books of knitting patterns and asked if I could grab them. They were a mixture of different clothing, so Mrs Chipley won't suspect I had an ulterior motive. When the nights draw in, I can keep warm knitting bootees and cardigans for the little one."

And so it begins, thought Gus. Roll on Tuesday when they could let everyone in on the secret. He could understand why he and Suzie were excited, and Jackie Ferris was pleased she would have a grandchild to hold at last. Why the world and his wife took such an interest was beyond him.

Gus gave the Reverend a cheery wave and returned indoors. He'd forgotten something. What was it he was supposed to do today? He grabbed the phone in the lounge and rang the Fox and Hounds. He was lucky; they could offer him a table at eight o'clock. Now he could relax and run through the day's events and plan what should follow in the morning.

Suzie breezed through the gateway at twenty past seven. Vicky had shown a slight improvement since her previous visit. Although there wasn't time for a complete account, as she needed to shower and change, Gus heard the details as he drove them to the pub.

"I would have driven," said Suzie when they were waiting for their meal. "You could have had a drink."

"You drove to Swindon and back after a long day, sweetheart," said Gus. "I can have a drink at the weekend."

"How did your interviews go?" asked Suzie.

"The case turned on its head during the second interview," said Gus. "Luke and Blessing excelled themselves. I'm confident we know our killer, but catching up with him could be tricky. Also, the Hub could add to our list of victims. Once that happens, the equivalent of the FBI will arrive in town, and we locals will stand aside while they take the glory."

Their main courses arrived, and conversation ceased. As Suzie scanned the desserts board for something she could sensibly order, Gus gave her the updated highlights of the Chaloner case.

"Thursday evening, and you're wrapping up another case, Gus Freeman," said Suzie, shaking her head. "Does nothing ever turn sour for you?"

"I rescued a chicken wrap from Kenneth's office on Monday," he said. "A slice of Kassie's summer berry cake was fine when I enjoyed it with a coffee on Tuesday afternoon, but the wrap was history. I can't win every time."

"I know," said Suzie. "It's galling when you start a case, and it becomes much larger than you ever imagined. Nobody could have foreseen that. Geoff will have no choice but to call in a major investigation team capable of handling the cases of multiple victims across the country."

"I shudder to think of the number of trips Jones made into mainland Europe," said Gus. "There's only one saving grace."

"What's that?" asked Suzie.

"If I'm right, we will confine the murders to November,"

"I don't think I fancy a sweet," said Suzie. "Can we order coffee and then go home?"

"Your wish is my command," said Gus.

Friday, 7 September 2018

GUS AND SUZIE went through their routine in the morning. As Suzie turned into the London Road HQ, Gus flashed his lights and continued towards the office. Neil, Blessing, and Luke had arrived before him. Alex and Lydia arrived in the car park just as Gus was locking his car door.

"Another glorious morning, guv," said Lydia.

"It's certainly bright, Lydia," said Gus.

"My suit's still at the dry cleaner's, guv," she grinned.

"What are we expecting this morning, guv?" asked Alex.

"We can't expect too much from Divya and the Hub," said Gus as they entered the lift. "They will need time to interrogate such an extended period. As for the international search, that will take time even to organise, let alone produce results."

"We're not out of Europe yet, guv," said Alex. "I hope their co-operation on finding a serial killer wouldn't get mired in petty squabbles. If that's what we're facing."

The others were chatting when they exited the lift.

"I'll call Eve Chaloner and ask about the bike, guv," said Blessing.

"Neil just raised a valid point, guv," said Luke. "Is it possible young Stan had another way of monitoring what was going on at the garage?"

"In what way, Neil?" asked Gus.

"The first-floor layout of those terraced houses on Ponting Street is common, guv. The larger bedroom is at the rear, so a parent could sleep during the day if he worked shifts. That means young Stan's bedroom overlooked the street."

"A camera? Would today's technology allow Stan to

view Ponting Street at the times he was interested in while he worked in the UK?"

"Without a doubt, guv," said Neil. "Luke and I wanted to take a trip to Swindon. What do you think?"

"No need to warn Stan Jones senior you're on your way," said Gus. "He'll be home."

Luke and Neil got ready to leave.

"Take Stan upstairs with you and ask him if he minds you having a look around."

"What are we looking for, guv?" asked Luke. "Apart from a hidden camera."

"The power source. Get Stan to switch it off if it's still operating. Then check the drawers or under the bed for anything that shouldn't be there."

"Like a Miami Cuban Link chain," said Blessing. "Twenty inches long, four millimetres wide, in twenty-two-carat gold with a box lock clasp."

"Trophies," said Lydia.

"It wouldn't surprise me," said Gus.

Luke and Neil were on their way to the ground floor.

"What are the odds, guv?" asked Alex.

"I don't think they'll find any trophies in Stan's bedroom, Alex," said Gus. "It's far more likely he'd keep them by him to look at from time to time. So instead, they'll be in the cab of his truck. Will the camera be operational if there was one? Probably not, but I bet they find evidence of one having been there. It answers several questions."

"When was the last time you investigated a case like this, guv?" asked Alex.

"A possible serial killer, Alex?" said Gus. "This is my first. Murder is rare in Wiltshire. Moreover, a serial killer is as common as snow in July."

"It hurts not to get the chance to see the case through to the end, guv," said Lydia.

"If either of you wants that opportunity, you need to spread your wings and fly from this nest," said Gus.

Blessing ended a phone call, and Gus saw her give one of her trademark punches in the air. A left-right combination, if he wasn't mistaken.

"Eve Chaloner had an old bicycle in her garage, I presume?"

"Yes, guv. Eve couldn't bring herself to throw it out. It's ready for collection when the next murder squad takes over the case. I remembered another loose end we hadn't dealt with."

"The safe?" asked Gus. Blessing nodded. He hadn't forgotten.

"Eve was aware Richard had a safe at home, guv," said Blessing. "He had it moved from his house in Pinehurst when they moved in after the wedding."

"I suppose we should inform the correct authorities," said Gus.

"I believed Eve when she told us they were trying for a baby, guv. When I asked whether the safe's contents helped her decide to stay home rather than look for a job after Richard died, Eve admitted the truth. She was shocked when she opened it and found over twenty thousand pounds inside."

"Leave that to me, DC Umeh," said Gus. "I'll mull it over, and decide what would be for the best."

"Got it, guv," said Blessing.

"Let's update the Freeman Files," said Gus, "and wait for news."

Lydia fetched coffees at ten. Alex's phone rang at five minutes past.

He listened to the voice at the other end, took notes, and ended the call.

"Emma Fox, twenty-three, guv," he said. "They found her body on November the sixteenth in 2007 on an embankment beside the motorway. Police believed she died after leaving a truck stop on the M6 where she may have attempted to hitchhike south. Emma left home at eighteen, and the police could not identify her or contact her family for ten months. They eventually identified Emma through fingerprints. Death by strangulation. No forensic evidence recovered at the scene."

"Anything else, Alex?" asked Gus.

"The cashier from the nearest service station thought she remembered Emma wearing a distinctive silver necklace and pendant, with the head of a fox and its brush studded with red stones. I haven't received the photo of the victim yet, guv, but Divya said the resemblance was uncanny."

"Thank you, Alex," said Gus.

It was going to be a long day.

Monday, 10 September 2018

"THE START of another new week, guv," said Neil Davis.

It surprised Gus to find anyone in the office. He'd left the bungalow thirty minutes earlier than usual. Suzie was only just making her way to the shower.

"I thought when we left here on Friday afternoon, I'd put everything to bed, Neil," said Gus. "While I worked on the allotment yesterday afternoon, I thought it best to run through our files one last time just in case we missed something. What brought you here so early?"

"Melody didn't have the best of nights," said Neil.

"Everything, okay with the baby?" asked Gus.

"I hope so, guv," said Neil. "The high temperatures earlier in the month didn't do Melody any favours. I was wide awake at six o'clock, so I thought, blow it, I will not get back to sleep before the alarm. If I drove here while the roads were quiet, I could start clearing the decks ready for our next case."

"Good idea," said Gus.

"By the way, I bumped into Rick Chalmers on Friday night, guv," said Neil.

"Did you take Melody for a meal?" asked Gus.

"No, guv. I met up with a couple of mates for a few cold beers. We were in the Silk Mercer in Devizes when Rick wandered in, alone."

Gus wondered whether Rick and Vera ever saw one another these days.

"How was he?"

"Rick had plenty to say, as usual, guv, but Friday night wasn't the right time or place for work. He's spent the past six weeks undercover."

"It seems to be the role that suits him best," said Gus. "Unsocial hours, with plenty of scope for fast food and casual relationships."

"Harsh, guv," said Neil. "Rick wouldn't go into detail in front of my mates, but he spoke to DS Mercer after he returned to London Road from this office in mid-July. The boss sent him to join a task force from Avon & Somerset Police. Rick's involvement in the undercover assignment ended on Thursday evening, and he delivered his report in person to DS Mercer on Friday afternoon."

"I'm intrigued, Neil," said Gus. "Any idea where Geoff Mercer might send Rick next?"

"Rick's on holiday for a week, guv," said Neil. "The boss told him to recharge his batteries and prepare to return to the seaside."

"Chasing illegal immigrants again," said Gus. "I don't envy him that job. But at least the weather's fine. Did he give a hint to where Avon & Somerset had him working undercover?"

"Rick said he thought it might interest you, guv," said Neil.

Gus heard the lift return to the ground floor. The rest of the team was on the way.

"Any idea where Rick's spending his week of relaxation?" he asked.

"He's got a flat somewhere in Devizes, guv," said Neil.

Alex Hardy and Lydia Logan Barre exited the lift and crossed the room to their desks.

"Morning, guv," said Lydia.

"Did we miss something?" asked Alex.

"No, Alex," said Gus, "Nothing further yet. Neil and I couldn't sleep. We were just chatting about Rick Chalmers."

"I saw him on Friday night," said Neil. "Alex, you know where his flat is, don't you?"

"I picked him up on the way to the Hub when we worked on the Grant Burnside case," said Alex. "A tad ambitious to call it a flat, it was more of a tip."

Luke Sherman and Blessing Umeh were next to arrive together. They were deep in conversation, and Lydia could tell Blessing had plenty to tell Luke. Jamie Barnes-Trewick was the chief topic, no doubt.

"Now everyone's here," said Gus. "Neil has offered to get the office ready for the next case. Can the rest of you double-check everything we added to our files last week, please? I would prefer to spend two hours ensuring we haven't dropped the ball rather than having our reputation shredded by the Chief Constable. When he passes the case on, he can be confident we did everything by the book."

"Got it, guv," said Alex.

Gus checked his mobile phone. Yes, he had Rick's number. Something told him Rick would enjoy a chat.

"Did I wake you?" he asked when Rick finally answered.

Neil grinned as he passed Gus's desk with the street maps of Swindon.

Thirty seconds later, Gus ended the call.

"Give me the address of that tip, Alex. I'm collecting Rick in half an hour. He suggested I bought him breakfast."

"That means he hasn't got a clean mug to get you a coffee, guv," said Lydia. "I don't know how people can live that way."

"He's a good copper," said Gus. "That score's highly in my book. Neil thinks Rick has something I'd like to hear. Alex, can you do me a favour? There's no sense in me returning to the office."

"I understand, guv," said Alex. "After we've cross-checked everything on the Chaloner case, I'll deliver the files to London Road. Vera Butler can hand them over when you arrive for your meeting with the Chief Constable. If Divya calls with news, I'll phone it through."

"You read my mind, Alex," said Gus as he headed for the lift.

It promised to be another warm, sunny day. Gus threw his jacket onto the passenger seat of the Focus. He wouldn't need it until his lunchtime session with Kenneth Truelove. If only he could risk opening his windows again.

Thirty minutes later, he parked in a side street near the

Leisure Centre in Devizes. Gus thought it ironic that Rick lived so close, considering his love of unhealthy grub and alcohol. However, Gus didn't have to get out of the car; because soon Rick appeared on the doorstep, slammed the door behind him, and strolled around to the passenger side.

"Mind my jacket," said Gus, grabbing it before Rick slumped into the seat beside him.

"Sorry, guv," said Rick. "Do you know Times Square?"

"A big place in New York, yes, I've heard of it. Why?"

"Not that one. It's in the Market Place, guv," said Rick. "They do a substantial breakfast."

"I take it you've continued to enjoy your break since Friday night when you bumped into Neil?"

"I've been home every night, guv, honest," said Rick. "I hoped to spend Saturday night elsewhere, but that fell through."

"A friend with benefits?" asked Gus.

"A reputation, guv. I ought to have known better," said Rick. "I spotted her on the other side of the room in the Cavalier, on Eastleigh Road. I think you know it?"

Gus nodded. He'd spent an hour there with Terry Davis on the day Neil's father died. It wasn't the sort of pub where Vera Butler spent a night out.

"Neil warned me off, but you know how it is," said Rick.

"I'm not sure I do, Rick," said Gus. "If Neil warned you off, it can't have been anyone I might have had in mind. We're talking about a young WPC, I suppose?"

"Amelia Cranston," said Rick. "She was with a group of girls her age. I didn't see any blokes with them. So, I bought Amelia a drink and started chatting. Her friends left us in the Cavalier and went into town. After closing time, we went back to her place. I had been drinking since lunchtime. That was my excuse, but it carried little weight with Ms Cranston."

"It happens to the best of us, Rick," said Gus.

"I walked back to my flat on Bridewell Street and was in bed before midnight. When it gets around the locker rooms at London Road, I'll be a laughing stock."

"It takes two to tango, Rick," said Gus. "Anyway, I didn't drive here this morning to discuss your love life or lack of it. Neil thought you had something of interest to tell me."

"Sorry, guv," said Rick. "I need a coffee first."

Gus parked by the Wharf Theatre, and they took a four-minute walk to Times Square.

Rick ordered the largest breakfast on offer and two coffees. The waitress came straight back with the coffees and then went about her business.

"Does the date Sunday the twenty-fifth of May ring a bell, guv?" he asked, leaning forward and keeping his voice low.

"Four years ago?" asked Gus. Rick nodded.

"That was the day Grant Burnside got shot out at Cheney Manor Industrial Estate," said Rick. "His son, Gary, was with him as well as his muscle men, Drewett and Hodge. They tortured and killed a guy called Howard Todd. Todd worked for the gang but skimmed a percentage off the top on drug deals he made on their behalf."

"Someone shot Grant as he sat outside the warehouse unit," said Gus. "Whoever it was had been on the roof watching proceedings. My team reviewed the original investigation but could not name the sniper. What we discovered was that people spotted a red-haired man working in adjoining warehouse units."

"Then, on the twelfth of July, we went for a drive in the

countryside with Neil and Luke," said Rick. "We both know how that ended."

"How does this relate to the undercover work you've just completed?" asked Gus. "A man like Grant Burnside attracted attention in the media. Theo Hickerton, who ran the original investigation at Gablecross, reckoned Grant Burnside believed he was invincible. He intimidated potential witnesses, threatened their families, and punished anyone who crossed him. He thought Grant made too many enemies, and it was only a matter of time before someone killed him."

"I think when you spoke with that guy Curran from the National Crime Agency, it became apparent someone other than the authorities was keeping tabs on Burnside and others."

"That was a meeting I'll never forget," said Gus. "Where does Curran fit into this? He warned me off investigating the matter further."

The waitress arrived with a large plate of fried food, and Rick licked his lips.

"Can I have another cup of coffee, please?" he asked her. He looked at Gus, who shook his head.

"As you pointed out, guv," said Rick, grabbing a large bottle of tomato ketchup, "if someone had their eye on Burnside, he didn't make it difficult to work out he was a career criminal who never paid for his crimes. In 2010, a jury cleared him of the murder of Spencer Curtis, a forty-four-year-old gang member stabbed to death near Wroughton. In 2013, a shooting happened in front of at least four people at a snooker club in Swindon. Theo Hickerton couldn't find anyone to say what they witnessed. They charged Grant Burnside with having blasted Blake Dixon in the chest at point-blank range with a sawn-off shotgun.

Dixon was a thirty-seven-year-old drug dealer on the night-club circuit. Yet again, Burnside walked from court a free man."

"Oh, he was guilty on each occasion," said Gus. "The problem Gablecross faced was finding someone to speak out against the Burnsides or stay alive long enough to reach court if they did."

"The surveillance team I got seconded to were sitting on that manor house, or whatever it was, deep in the country-side," said Rick.

"Larcombe Manor," said Gus. "I remember it well. So how did Avon & Somerset get clearance?"

"Who says they asked?" said Rick. "The guys I worked with told me it was personal. Two of their senior officers defected to the charity several years ago, and then Callum Wood joined the exodus."

"That was the man who met us in the driveway," said Gus. "then suggested we turn around and disappear."

"We set up our observation posts in a wooded area, south of the main buildings. As you know, the road we arrived on allowed us to see the upper floors of the manor house from the entrance, but the land falls away into the valley. We had a better view of what was happening in the other buildings from our hide."

"Were you disguised as birdwatchers?" asked Gus.

"Not quite," said Rick. "We used the most sophisticated kit available to a county force, and apart from satellite images, we couldn't have got much better."

"Who were you watching, and why?"

"David Scott, ex-SAS sergeant," said Rick. "A red-haired man of fifty. Scott was a fiery beggar in his youth. A difference of opinion with a senior officer led to the SAS and Scott parting company. He had his arguments with plenty of others over the years. His friends said it was because he didn't suffer fools gladly."

"That's the who, now the why," said Gus.

"A bit of background first. We heard from colleagues in Somerset that a body turned up buried in a field scheduled for a solar farm. It was another SAS sergeant by the name of Dickerson. The body had been in the ground for three to four years. The last time anyone saw Dickerson alive was in September 2014 in Rotherham. Scott and Dickerson served in Iraq together a decade earlier with Task Force Black. They were with D Section of the SAS and worked with the American Delta Force in covert operations against Al Qaeda and other insurgents. They had a three-word motto—find, fix, finish."

"Find an insurgent, fix a time and place, and finish with a raid to take the suspect out."

"Got it in one," said Rick. "If only we could do it that way."

"Dangerous work in treacherous conditions," said Gus.

"Booby-trapped buildings and vehicles," said Rick, "plus grenades wired to doors and windows. Dickerson was supposed to clear the way for another team to move through. Instead, he signalled everything was okay, and two men died when an IED exploded. Scott blamed Dickerson."

"The Iraq War was a decade ago," said Gus. "What happened in 2014?"

"We believe Scott and others linked to the manor house carried out an operation in Yorkshire. The three little words we were discussing would sum it up. The targets weren't insurgents but men guilty of grooming young girls and sexually exploiting them. They also trafficked underage girls to several major cities across the country. Several of these men disappeared. The person who planned and helped execute their disappearance is dead. Avon & Somerset believe they have enough evidence to charge Scott. What that charge should be is up to the Crown Prosecution Service."

"How does that impact on the Grant Burnside business?" asked Gus.

"You found evidence of a sniper on the roof of the building, opposite the spot where Burnside died. A witness saw a red-haired man in the vicinity of the ladder at the side of that building. The sniper crossed rough ground near a lake to reach the industrial estate. We have obtained images of Scott in Rotherham in September 2014, which Avon & Somerset believe are of the same man. The clincher came from what happened in early June 2014. Larcombe Manor has a hospital on-site, heaven knows why, but Scott went to the Royal United in Bath because of a lung infection. The doctor diagnosed Legionnaire's disease. They thought Scott must have ingested droplets of water carrying the bacteria when he spent time near stagnant water. That puts him squarely in the Cheney Manor area at the end of May. Scott was the man who killed Grant Burnside. As for Dickerson, if he met Scott in Yorkshire and knowing their history, Avon & Somerset believe Scott and others brought Dickerson to Larcombe Manor and killed him or ferried him south to dispose of the body."

"How did Dickerson die?" asked Gus.

"Blunt force trauma to the side of the head. The pathologist thought it resembled a wound caused by a rifle butt."

"Your undercover work might have allowed us to put a tick against the only case we weren't able to solve," said Gus. "Thanks, Rick. I look forward to hearing officially from Geoff Mercer. I presume he's not sitting on your report until the dust settles so he can bury it?"

"The boys at Portishead have a way to go before getting

Scott to court," said Rick, using his last piece of bread to wipe the plate clean. "They have a retired High Court judge on the payroll at the Manor."

"I'll keep an eye out for an update on the David Scott case," said Gus.

"Rusty," said Rick. "He answers to Rusty."

Epilogue

GUS DROVE Rick back to his flat and dropped him at the door.

"Take a sweater with you when you go to the seaside chasing those illegal immigrants, Rick," he said. "The evenings are getting chilly. I'll keep in touch."

Only a matter of minutes later, Gus turned into the London Road car park. He skipped up the steps to the front door and made his way to Reception. When he reached the mezzanine, Vera Butler nodded towards the folders on her desk.

"Alex Hardy dropped these in ten minutes ago, Gus. Geoff is free if you want to pop in. Kenneth is with the PCC and won't be available until after lunch."

"Many thanks, Vera," said Gus, gathering the files without stopping for a chat. He tapped on Geoff Mercer's door.

"Come in," said Geoff. "Gus, it's usually good to see you, but Vera suggested I looked at these files before you got here."

Geoff handed Gus a folder with two sheets of paper inside.

ON NOVEMBER THE NINTH, 2010, a woman's body was found in a storage cupboard on an abandoned industrial site near Smethwick. She had been suffocated. Molly Phelps, twenty-two years old, had been dead for several days. Originally from Paisley in Scotland, Molly's parents said their daughter was trying to get a lift home for the weekend and never arrived. The photograph they gave the police showed Molly wearing a gold choker chain with a cross. Police found no jewellery with the body.

GUS STARED at the photo of the young girl. There was no mistake. The hair colouring was different, but Stan Jones would have been reminded of Tara Laing the second he set eyes on the poor girl. Gus turned over the sheet.

ON NOVEMBER TWENTIETH, 2013, a dog walker found Sammy Yendall, twenty-two, near Wentwood Forest in Monmouthshire. The similarities were there again. Gus sighed. What did he take as a trophy this time? The cause of death differed from the others, and the violence was more significant. Sammy had been struck several times with a hammer or similar object on the skull and about her face. The killer wanted to obliterate her facial features. Her family, from Newport, said she always wore a charm bracelet by Pandora that at last count had eleven charms.

"ALEX RECEIVED MORE information after you left the office, Gus," said Geoff. "There's another sheet here he left with Vera."

Luke and Neil had visited young Stan's bedroom in Ponting Street. The camera itself had gone, but the window sill held evidence someone had fixed something there for a lengthy period. Stan's father hadn't been inside his son's room since he was thirteen.

Luke checked the bedside table drawer, under the bed, and both inside and on top of the wardrobe. He found no sign of any trophies. Neil had taken Stan Jones downstairs to look at the mail awaiting his son's return. His subscription for the Swindon Advertiser would be due for renewal in mid-November.

"GRIM READING, GUS," said Geoff.

"We need to find Jones before he strikes again," said Gus.

"We owe it to any girl out there who reminds him of Tara Laing. They deserve to be allowed to look forward to a normal November."

Next in The Freeman Files series

vinci-books.com/intothesunlight

A young woman's murder. A cold case reopened. A race against time.

When a young Lithuanian woman's body is discovered in a ditch, the Wiltshire Crime Review Team, led by the tenacious Gus Freeman, takes on the perplexing cold case. With each new lead, the team is drawn deeper into a labyrinth of mystery, racing against time to bring justice to Danute and her loved ones.

Turn the page for a free preview…

Into The Sunlight: Chapter One

Friday, 7 September 2018

Gus and Suzie went through their regular routine in the morning. Gus flashed his lights as Suzie turned into the London Road HQ and continued towards the office. Neil, Blessing, and Luke had arrived before him. As Gus locked his car door, Alex and Lydia entered the car park.

"Another glorious morning, guv," said Lydia when she got out of her Mini.

"It's certainly bright, Lydia," said Gus.

"My suit's still at the dry cleaner's, guv," she grinned.

"What are we expecting this morning, guv?" asked Alex.

"We can't hope for too much from Divya and the Hub," said Gus as they entered the lift. "They will need time to carry out search routines over an extended period. An international search will take even longer to arrange, let alone produce results."

"We're not out of Europe yet, guv," said Alex. "I hope

their co-operation in finding a serial killer wouldn't get mired in petty squabbles. If that's what we're facing."

The others were chatting when they exited the lift.

Blessing Umeh notified Gus she was about to call Eve Chaloner. They needed to follow up on Richard Chaloner's bicycle. Neil wondered whether Stan Jones Junior could monitor what was going on at the garage via a camera in what had been his bedroom.

Gus knew tying up these inconsequential loose ends wasn't vital, but it might add icing to the cake. So he suggested Luke and Neil drive to Swindon on Monday to check Neil's theory without antagonising Stan's father.

Blessing reminded Neil to look for the gold chain the killer had stolen; Lydia pointed out there could be other items young Stan might have kept as trophies. Souvenirs of what he saw as good times in his life. Gus felt it more likely they would be with him in the cab of his truck.

"When was the last time you investigated a case like this, guv?" asked Alex.

"A possible serial killer, Alex?" said Gus. "This is my first. Murder is rare in Wiltshire. Moreover, a serial killer is as common as snow in July."

"It hurts not to get the chance to see the case through to the end, guv," said Lydia.

"That goes for me too, guv," said Alex.

"If either of you wants the opportunity, you need to spread your wings and fly from this nest," said Gus.

Blessing soon received confirmation that Richard's bicycle had been returned after the original forensics crew finished their work. Eve Chaloner told her she hadn't been able to throw the bicycle out.

"It can stay where it is, for now, Blessing," said Gus.

"Whichever Murder Investigation Team gets assigned to the case can decide what happens next."

"I believed Eve when she told us they were trying for a baby, guv," said Blessing. "When I asked whether the safe's contents helped her decide to stay home rather than look for a job after Richard died, Eve admitted the truth. However, it was a shock to open the safe and find over twenty thousand pounds inside she knew nothing about."

"Leave it to me, DC Umeh," said Gus. "I'll mull it over and decide what would be for the best."

"Got it, guv," said Blessing.

"Let's update the Freeman Files," said Gus, "and wait for news."

Lydia fetched coffee at ten. Alex's phone rang five minutes past.

He listened to the voice at the other end, took notes, and ended the call.

"Emma Fox, twenty-three, guv," he said. "They found her body on November the sixteenth, 2007, on an embankment beside the motorway. Police believed she died after leaving a truck stop on the M6 where she may have attempted to hitchhike south. Emma left home at eighteen, and the police could not identify her or contact her family for ten months. They eventually identified Emma through fingerprints. Death by strangulation. No forensic evidence was recovered at the scene."

"Anything else, Alex?" asked Gus.

"The cashier from the nearest service station thought she remembered Emma wearing a distinctive silver necklace and pendant, with the head of a fox and its brush studded with red stones. I haven't received a photo of the victim yet, guv, but Divya said the resemblance to Tara Laing was uncanny."

"Thank you, Alex," said Gus.

It promised to be a long day.

Monday, 10 September 2018

"The start of another new week, guv," said Neil Davis.

It surprised Gus to find anyone in the office. He'd left the bungalow thirty minutes earlier than usual. Suzie had only just been making her way to the shower.

"I thought when we left here on Friday afternoon, I'd put everything to bed, Neil," said Gus. "While I worked on the allotment yesterday afternoon, I thought it best to run through our files one last time in case we missed something. What brought you here so early?"

"Melody didn't have the best of nights, guv," said Neil.

"Everything okay with the baby?" asked Gus.

"I hope so, guv," said Neil. "The high temperatures earlier in the month didn't do Melody any favours. I was wide awake at six o'clock, so I thought, blow it, I won't get back to sleep before the alarm. I could start clearing the decks for our next case if I drove here while the roads were quiet."

"Good idea," said Gus.

"By the way, I bumped into Rick Chalmers on Friday night, guv," said Neil.

"Did you take Melody out for a meal?" asked Gus.

"No, guv. I met up with a couple of mates for a few cold beers. We were in the Silk Mercer in Devizes when Rick wandered in alone."

Gus wondered whether Rick and Vera ever saw one another these days.

"How was he?"

"Rick had plenty to say, as usual, guv, but Friday night wasn't the right time or place for work. He'd spent the past six weeks undercover."

"It seems to be the role that suits him best," said Gus. "Unsocial hours, with plenty of scope for fast food and casual relationships."

"Harsh, guv," said Neil. "Rick wouldn't go into detail in front of my mates, but he spoke to DS Mercer after he returned to London Road from this office in mid-July. The boss sent him to join a task force from Avon & Somerset Police. Rick's involvement in the undercover assignment ended Thursday evening, and he delivered his report in person on Friday afternoon."

"I'm intrigued, Neil," said Gus. "Any idea where Geoff Mercer might send Rick next?"

"Rick's on holiday for a week, guv," said Neil. "The boss told him to recharge his batteries and prepare to return to the seaside."

"Chasing illegal immigrants again," said Gus. "I don't envy him that job. But at least the weather's fine. Did he give a hint to where Avon & Somerset had him working undercover?"

"Rick said he thought it might interest you, guv," said Neil.

Gus heard the lift return to the ground floor. The rest of the team was on the way.

"Any idea where Rick's spending his week of relaxation?" he asked.

"He's got a flat somewhere in Devizes, guv," said Neil.

Alex Hardy and Lydia Logan Barre exited the lift and crossed the room to their desks.

"Morning, guv," said Lydia.

"Did we miss something?" asked Alex.

"No, Alex," said Gus. "Nothing further yet. Neil and I couldn't sleep. We were chatting about Rick Chalmers."

"I saw him on Friday night," said Neil. "Alex, you know where his flat is, don't you?"

"I picked him up on the way to the Hub when we worked on the Grant Burnside case," said Alex. "A tad ambitious to call it a flat; it was more of a tip."

Luke Sherman and Blessing Umeh were next to arrive. They were deep in conversation, and Lydia could tell Blessing had plenty to tell Luke. Jamie Barnes-Trewick was the chief topic, no doubt. Luke seemed more animated than usual, too.

"Now everyone's here," said Gus. "Neil has offered to prepare the office for the next case. Can the rest of you double-check everything we added to our files last week, please?"

"Sure, guv," said Lydia. "No problem."

"I would prefer to spend two hours ensuring we haven't dropped the ball rather than having our reputation shredded by the Chief Constable," added Gus. "When he hands the case onto MCIT, he can be confident we did everything by the book."

"Got it, guv," said Alex.

Gus checked his mobile phone. Yes, he had Rick's number. Something told him Rick would enjoy a chat.

Luke and Neil set off for Swindon to check for the hidden camera. After a quick phone call to Rick, Gus drove to Devizes twenty minutes later.

Their meeting took place over an extended brunch in a town centre café. After Gus dropped Rick back home, he headed for London Road. At last, there was a light on the horizon. Rick's undercover work might have allowed them to put a tick against the only case the Crime Review Team hadn't solved. Gus thanked Rick and looked forward to hearing officially from Geoff Mercer that Avon & Somerset Police at Portishead had removed any obstacles preventing them from getting Rusty Scott to court.

Minutes after leaving Rick, Gus turned into the London Road car park. He skipped up the steps to the front door and made his way to reception. When he reached the mezzanine, Vera Butler nodded towards a pile of folders on her desk.

"Alex Hardy dropped these off ten minutes ago. Gus. Geoff is free if you want to pop in. Kenneth is with the PCC and won't be available until after lunch."

"Many thanks, Vera," said Gus, gathering the files without stopping for a chat. He tapped on Geoff Mercer's door.

"Come in," said Geoff. "Gus, it's usually good to see you, but Vera suggested I looked at a couple of these files before you got here."

Geoff handed Gus a folder with two sheets of paper inside.

Gus studied the first sheet. On November the ninth, 2010, a woman's body was found in a storage cupboard on an abandoned industrial site near Smethwick. She had been suffocated. Molly Phelps, twenty-two years old, had been dead for several days. Originally from Paisley in Scotland, Molly's parents said their daughter was trying to get a lift home for the weekend and never arrived. The photograph they gave the police showed Molly wearing a gold choker chain with a cross. Police found no jewellery with the body.

Gus stared at the photo of the young girl. There was no mistake. The hair colouring was different, but Stan Jones would have been reminded of Tara Laing the second he set eyes on the poor girl. Gus turned over the second sheet.

On November the twentieth, 2013, a dog walker found Sammy Yendall, twenty-two, near Wentwood Forest in Monmouthshire. The similarities were there again. Gus sighed. What did he take as a trophy this time? The cause of death differed from the others, and the violence was more significant. Sammy had been struck several times with a hammer or similar object on the skull and about her face. The killer wanted to obliterate her facial features. Her family, from Newport, said she always wore a charm bracelet by Pandora that, at last count, had eleven charms.

"Alex received more information just before he left the office, Gus," said Geoff. "There's another note here he left with Vera."

Luke and Neil had visited young Stan's bedroom on Ponting Street. The camera itself had gone, but the window sill held evidence someone had fixed something there for a lengthy period. Stan's father hadn't been inside his son's room since he was thirteen.

Luke had checked the bedside table drawer under the bed, inside and on top of the wardrobe. He found no sign of any trophies. Neil had taken Stan Jones downstairs to look at the mail awaiting his son's return. His subscription to the Swindon Advertiser would be due for renewal in mid-November.

"Grim reading, Gus," said Geoff.

"We need to find Jones before he strikes again," said Gus.

"We owe it to any girl who reminds him of Tara Laing. They deserve to be allowed to look forward to a normal November."

"Everything's ready on the Chaloner case in these files

when Kenneth's free," said Gus. "Who do you think will get the pleasure of making the headlines?"

"They've got plenty to choose from these days, Gus," said Geoff. "You know the Metropolitan Police have twenty-four teams for the capital. We wouldn't warrant many teams on our patch, so our Major Crime Investigation Team is a collaborative unit comprising officers and staff from Wiltshire, Gloucestershire, Avon, and Somerset Police areas. The unit's remit includes the investigation of Category A-C homicides throughout the tri-force areas."

"I wish I hadn't asked," said Gus.

"I guess it will be sent out of the county to one of our neighbours. Does that bother you?"

"Not at all," said Gus. "Our remit was to put a name to Richard Chaloner's killer. I'm confident we identified the guilty party. There was no sign in the original murder file to suggest we were hunting a serial killer. The trick cyclists will agonise over why Jones waited so long before taking revenge on the lad who threw the firework that scarred him. Would he have attacked the others in time? When Stan Jones is in custody, someone can pose the question."

"I see your point," said Geoff. "He went after girls who reminded him of Tara Laing. But am I being too optimistic? There's a three-year gap between the murders you've identified."

"Stan was due to marry Tara in November 2004," said Gus. "Jeanie, his mother, hung on for a year. He'd already left home by then but returned for her funeral. Maybe you're right, and the ghost wedding, followed by his mother's death, were two events he kept churning over in his head as he drove for hour after hour. Emma Fox could have been his first victim. But after that, why should he stop? If Jones's anger gets the better of him every three years, then this November, he'll target another Tara look-alike. My worry is he gets angry several days before Halloween, regardless of the year."

"God help us if there are half a dozen more bodies out there," said Geoff.

Gus looked at his watch.

"How long before the Chief Constable can escape the clutches of the Police and Crime Commissioner?"

"These meetings tend to run on," sighed Geoff. "Ah, I see where this is heading. As Kenneth's with the PCC in an unscheduled meeting, Vera won't have cancelled the regular lunch order. I'll give her a shout, and she can bring the grub into my office."

"Do you know what he's lined up for us to tackle next?" Gus asked.

"Not the specifics," said Geoff. "You know what he's like. Kenneth wears his heart on his sleeve. Look at how he rescued Kassie Trotter from the perils of life on the streets."

"His faith in whatever denomination church he attends is commendable," said Gus. "Does that suggest we're heading for the seamier side of society on this occasion? Kenneth and his wife are more interested than most in the young women who fall through the safety net."

"It appears so," said Geoff. "On Friday afternoon, we chatted before we went our separate ways to drive home. He'd been reading another of those reports on his desk you ribbed him about last week."

"Never a good idea on an empty stomach," said Gus.

"Sorry," said Geoff. "I'll call Vera now."

Geoff made the call.

"That was lucky," he said. "Vera had just left to take her thirty-minute break. Thank goodness Kassie picks up her calls. We're okay. She'll be right in."

Gus could hear Kassie singing as she pushed her trolley along the dark corridor towards Geoff's office. He wanted to learn what Kenneth had been reading, but Kassie did enjoy a chat. Whatever it was could wait a few minutes.

The door swung open, and Kassie entered.

"I've taken a liberty, Mr Mercer," she said, giving Gus a cheeky grin. "You would have only made a pig of yourself trying to eat the Chief Constable's share as well as your own. So, I let the young lad in reception have Kenneth's baguette."

"As long as I have my usual order, that's fine," said Geoff.

"You can manage two wraps, can't you, Mr Freeman?"

"If I must, Kassie," said Gus. "What's on the secret menu this week? Will there be something scrummy to collect on my way back to the office?"

"I had another bash at making cream horns," said Kassie. "They look good, even if I say so myself."

"I'll take one back with me," said Gus.

"Might I have two?" asked Geoff.

"Sorry, Mr Mercer," said Kassie. "I only have one spare now that Mr Freeman's agreed to give them another try."

"What happened to Kenneth's cake?" asked Gus.

"The lad on reception's got it, I bet," moaned Geoff.

"Are we talking about the comedian I met a few weeks ago?" asked Gus. "I didn't think you fancied him."

"I don't," said Kassie. "But if I feed him up, he might do, at a pinch."

"Young men around here must feel like turkeys at Christmas," said Geoff.

"Enjoy your lunch, you two," said Kassie. "I'll see you later, Mr Freeman."

With that, Kassie, together with her heart and lovebird tattoos, had gone.

"I'll run through the content of Kenneth's reading material after we demolish this food," said Geoff. "Did you have a good weekend, Gus? Anything exciting planned this week, depending on where your next case takes you, of course?"

"Suzie and I spent a quiet weekend at the bungalow or the allotment," Gus said. "As for this week. I need time off on Wednesday afternoon."

"Interesting," said Geoff. "DI Ferris made the same request this morning, A couple of hours late on Wednesday afternoon, she said."

"Suzie didn't give any further details?" asked Gus.

Geoff Mercer shook his head.

"Then I'll await further instructions," said Gus.

"Fair enough," said Geoff. "No problem. I presume DS Hardy will take control while you're absent?"

"That's standard procedure," said Gus. "Have you heard any more from DS Sherman?"

"Not a whisper, Gus. Has he spoken to you?"

"We've not had much chance, but he did seem in a better mood this morning. So perhaps Luke and his partner got through the weekend without a blazing row for a change."

"It might pay you to take Luke on the early interviews in your next job. Then, he might open up away from the office. Someone has to go with you. You might as well use it to your advantage."

"I'll bear it in mind," said Gus. "Right. What was it that piqued Kenneth's paternal instinct?"

"Human trafficking," said Geoff. "Especially where these unfortunate souls end up. In the past decade, the number of people trafficked into the UK for sexual exploitation has risen. Ten years ago, a modest five hundred, three-quarters of whom were adults, but that number had doubled within four years."

"Still a relatively small number compared to other countries worldwide," said Gus.

"The numbers continued to rise," said Geoff, "and those were just the known victims."

"Where do the majority come from?" asked Gus.

"Many make the short trip from the Baltic States," said Geoff. "Some are from Russia and Eastern European countries, Ukraine, Romania, and Albania. Then, of course, others originate from Africa and South East Asia."

"No doubt there's a financial cost to this misery?" said Gus. "Criminal gangs have always been involved in this business. Any commodity that has value to them is fair game. So what are the gangs paying for these women?"

"Perhaps an average of five thousand pounds," said Geoff. "The girls work sixteen-hour days and are expected to service a client every thirty minutes."

"Why do these women come to this country?" asked Gus.

"They get lured here under false pretences, expecting to have a restaurant job or as a nanny," said Geoff. "Instead, they get moved around the country as money passes hands between the gangmasters. You might assume they only gravitate to the major cities. But the problem has grown so large they can turn up anywhere from Cornwall to Cumbria."

"After Terry Davis's murder, I visited Donna, one of his informants," said Gus. "A note Terry passed her helped put Culverhouse and Plunkett in the frame for the hit-and-run they tried to hide. Donna likes to tell people she runs a business in Devizes in the care sector. Several of her staff arrived in the county from those European countries you mentioned, but they're not exploited in the same way as those that fall into the hands of criminal gangs."

"It's a fine line, Gus," said Geoff. "As soon as more than one person uses the same premises to sell sex, we should act. I'll have to accept that Donna runs a care home until I can prove otherwise. I don't suppose you remember where it was?"

"It slipped my mind completely as soon as I left with the clue that Terry gave us," said Gus. "Was there a particular story in that report that got Kenneth agitated?"

"He spoke of a girl called Olga from Krakow," said Geoff. "She was seventeen and leaving school when she saw an advert online for a nanny. The couple claimed to have an eighteen-month-old daughter and wanted an au pair to live in. The story was that the wife wanted to return to work full-time. Olga replied to the advert, and weeks later, she flew into Exeter airport. The couple had paid for her passport, sent her a one-way plane ticket, and agreed to help her learn English. Olga thought everything was legit and looked forward to the experience. The wife collected her from the Arrivals area and led her to a people carrier outside the airport. They drove to a detached house in a leafy suburb where Olga was introduced to the husband."

"And the eighteen-month-old daughter?" asked Gus.

"She never existed. The couple took everything from Olga except the clothes she was wearing and locked her in an upstairs bedroom. Her nightmare had begun; no passport, money, or mobile phone. The husband told her she needed to work to repay the money. Olga asked about the baby, and the wife told her there were other ways she could earn enough money to pay them back. They forced Olga to call her parents to tell them she'd arrived safely and everything was fine. The wife held the phone while the husband held a knife to the poor girl's throat. Fifteen months later, Olga was spotted soliciting in the nightclub area near Little Castle and Bailey Street. The officers took her to a nearby café, and Olga revealed she was being put to work by an organised crime gang. The police soon learned that the couple who lured her to the UK had sold Olga to a local gang. Olga showed the police the house where she had originally lived and worked. The couple kept her in that bedroom twenty-four-seven for eight months."

"Nobody noticed numerous visitors?" asked Gus.

"They had chosen the property well," said Geoff. "It was the last house before an electricity sub-station, and there was plenty of passing traffic, but the driveway couldn't be seen from other houses on the road because of a bend and a row of leylandii."

"Were the couple still there?"

"No, but after months trawling through financial records and liaising with neighbouring forces, the couple were discovered in Wareham, Dorset. Further examination of mobile phones and computers seized at their new address showed they ran a highly organised operation for more than five years, trafficking vulnerable women, usually from mainland Europe. They targeted women who couldn't speak English and had no way of securing legal work in the UK. The wife uploaded profiles of the girls onto adult websites and after a while moved them around the country to carry out sex work."

"When they sold Olga to this other Devon-based gang, she went from the frying pan to the fire, I presume," said Gus.

"Olga said the couple used drugs to control her. Every day was a blur; then, one night, she tried to escape. Olga told the police she was heading for the railway line. They had passed it on the drive to the house from the airport. She just wanted to end the nightmare. When the husband caught her, he punched Olga half a dozen times in the stomach. The next night, Olga was driven from the house and dropped near the car wash at the back of a garage forecourt a few miles out of Exeter. Olga said she was ordered to wear a white blouse, a short black skirt, and knee-high white socks. She stood shivering in the dark, awaiting her fate. A van with tinted windows pulled into the parking bay beside her. The driver got out and went inside the garage shop. The passenger jumped out, bundled Olga through the van's side door, and told her to keep quiet. Minutes later, the van drove away from the forecourt. Olga had been moved on to another gang with girls in flats in Exeter city centre. She was expected to be available from six at night until six in the morning and earn a thousand pounds a night. If she didn't make enough money, the driver beat her."

"So, Olga suffered for a further seven months working for this gang?"

"Her torture ended when she left the café that night with the police. Olga is back with her family in Krakow, trying to rebuild her life. She was key to the investigation that led to the couple getting convicted under the Modern Slavery Act. They are now in prison. Work is ongoing to bring the other gang to the courts. They profit from the misery of others and show no regard for the welfare and wellbeing of the women they exploit."

"We have to celebrate every small success, I suppose," said Gus. "The gangs have accumulated so much clean cash they can afford the best legal representation. So it's hard to make charges stick."

Geoff and Gus sat quietly, drinking their coffees.

"Grace would have something to say if she found us spinning our wheels," said Gus.

"I blame the PCC," said Geoff. "He wants a lean, mean fighting machine, and then he whips our leader away at a minute's notice. So you're stuck here until Kenneth becomes available. It makes no sense to drive back to the office. As for me, perhaps I should throw you out and get on with that pile of paperwork in my in-tray. If I did, you could guarantee Kenneth would call me into his office before you reached the top of the stairs."

Gus heard singing in the corridor.

"Kassie's on her way," he said.

"Someone's made her life brighter," said Geoff. "A brave man, but not before time."

Kassie knocked but was through the door before an echo had a chance to escape.

"Vera will be back in five minutes," she said, "then I'll get a chance to enjoy thirty minutes of late summer sun myself. I brought your cream horns in person."

"Brilliant," said Geoff, licking his lips.

"You won't get this service every week," said Kassie. "It's just that the boss is back in his office. He asked whether I'd seen you two. I've taken his coffee in, so give it five minutes, and he'll expect you."

"Thanks, Kassie," said Geoff.

Gus inspected the white paper napkin contents as Kassie breezed out of the room. It looked tempting, but it could get messy. Discretion being the better part of valour, he decided to wait until he was in the Focus. Geoff Mercer had no such qualms; he was already wiping the excess puff pastry crumbs and sweet vanilla cream from his lips.

"I know," he said. "Don't give me that look. Christine

tuts if I have two chocolate digestive biscuits with a coffee on Sunday morning as a treat."

Gus wrapped his treat in the napkin and placed it on Geoff's desk.

"I'll pick it up when we've finished our meeting with Kenneth," he said. "Don't get any ideas."

Geoff was still grinning when his phone rang.

"That was Vera," said Geoff. "She's back from lunch, and Kenneth is ready and waiting."

Into The Sunlight: Chapter Two

Gus and Geoff took the short walk across the mezzanine to the Chief Constable's office. His door was open, and they could see Kenneth Truelove seated at his desk.

"Sorry for the delay, chaps. Come in," said Kenneth. "The PCC had a bee in his bonnet."

"Anything to concern us, sir?" asked Gus.

"I stopped listening after the first thirty minutes," said Kenneth, puffing out his cheeks. "It was the same old, same old. More, better, with less every day."

"We do what we can," said Gus.

"The PCC can hardly have a go at the Crime Review Team on that score, sir," said Geoff. "I've seen Gus's latest report. Did you have time to catch up with the Chaloner case yet?"

"Vera left a copy on my desk," said Kenneth. "That's as far as it got. I believe one of your team delivered it, Freeman. Where were you?"

"I was following up on the Burnside case with Rick Chalmers, sir. We had an early morning meeting in town."

It was early for Rick Chalmers, but Kenneth didn't need to hear the details.

"Any progress? Didn't you update me on that last week, Mercer?"

"I told you Chalmers had returned from his undercover spell with Avon & Somerset Police, sir. We agreed to let Rick have a week's leave, and then he will return to the South coast helping stem the flow of dodgy Channel crossings."

"He's your odd-job man, Mercer, isn't he? Chalmers always strikes me as another Terry Davis in the making. A detective with his finger on the pulse wherever he's put to work but with little drive or ambition to progress further. Sometimes it's better not to ask where they get the key pieces of information that crack a case."

"When I started as a DC at Bourne Hill," said Gus, "my first Sergeant told me every police station needed someone who did the dirty work. Someone prepared to rummage around in the muck looking for diamonds."

"I imagine you view those as the good old days, Freeman," said Kenneth. "I could not possibly comment."

"The days when dinosaurs ruled the earth, sir," said Gus. "We've come a long way since then, although not always in the right direction. Rick updated me on his recent team's progress on charging the man we believed responsible for the hit on Grant Burnside."

"Yes, Mercer did mention that. We must rely on Portishead to prepare a solid case. As for this folder in front of me. What do I need to know before I give it my full attention?"

"Richard Chaloner was killed by Stanley Jones, the thirty-seven-year-old son of a gentleman with the same name, who lives opposite Chaloner's garage on Ponting Street. The bare bones of the case were that when Jones was a young boy, Chaloner and his mates threw fireworks for a laugh on Bonfire Night, regardless of where they landed. Young Stanley suffered scarring of the face and hands in an incident in 1989."

"Twenty-odd years is a long time to wait," said Kenneth. "And murder seems an extreme way to get his own back. I sense there's more to it."

"Jones was engaged to be married when he was twenty-four, but the young lady, a Tara Laing, got cold feet," said Geoff Mercer. "By this time, Jones had taken a job as a truck driver. He travels throughout the UK and Europe. His visits to Ponting Street are rare, certainly since his mother died in 2005."

"Something had to give," said Kenneth. "A series of negative life events and this chap flipped; he identified Chaloner as the root cause of his misfortunes and shot him."

Geoff Mercer looked at Gus. If only it were that simple.

"We believe your first action should be to pass this case on, sir," said Geoff.

"Tara Laing might have triggered the first murder, sir," said Gus.

"The first? How many are there, for heaven's sake?"

"We can't answer that yet, sir," said Gus. "Jones suffered from being jilted, and then he lost his mother to cancer eighteen months later. Then, in November 2007, the body of a young woman, Emma Fox, was discovered on an embankment on the M6. We've compared photographs of Tara Laing and the twenty-three-year-old victim. They could be twins. The murder took place in November."

"DS Hardy also provided you with two additional murders that appear related, sir," said Geoff. "Vera would have dropped a folder onto the pile on your desk."

Kenneth flicked through the items at the top of the enormous pile.

"Got it," he said grimly. "Two more young women in the UK, two more murders which occurred in November. The photos on the sheets of paper in this folder suggest we're dealing with a serial killer. The similarities are undeniable. Unfortunately, as much as I would love for the Crime Review Team to trace Jones and bring him to justice, they don't have the resources. It's above the pay grade of the detectives under your wing, Freeman. I'm sorry."

"We understand, sir," said Gus. "DS Mercer and I are concerned we haven't identified every victim in this expanded case yet. So we involved the Hub last Friday. Divya Yadav is searching for matches between November 2005 and 2017."

"She's hunting for young women with the physical appearance of this Laing woman," said the Chief Constable. "I have no problem with the Hub's resources getting used on that task; it's why they're there. You say this Jones character travels in Europe too?"

"He does. We thought if the contact with the Major Crime Investigation Team came from you, sir, they would be more likely to get a wiggle on," said Gus. "November isn't far away, and I want Jones arrested before he can add another Tara Laing look-alike to his list."

"Fair enough. I'll handle that," said Kenneth. "I'll have a word with Mrs Yadav too and inform MCIT we should be able to identify the scope of the UK murders in a matter of hours. What about the attack on Chaloner, though? That was two years ago now. You mentioned he was with other teenage tearaways back in 1989. Have any of those men been attacked since 2005?"

"No, sir," said Geoff Mercer. "I've contacted Gablecross

and asked for the necessary surveillance during November to keep them out of harm's way."

"I would hope Jones was in custody before we get that far, Mercer," said Kenneth.

"He's clever, sir," said Gus. "At least three young women plus Richard Chaloner died without either investigation into their deaths having any success. He's never left discernible DNA at the scene. Until we worked on the Chaloner murder file last week, nobody had established a link between Jones and these random killings in three separate parts of the country."

"Did Tara Laing come from Swindon?" asked Kenneth. "Have you asked Gablecross to provide her with protection, Mercer?"

"Tara Laing had an interesting career after she ditched Stan Jones," said Gus. "Ms Laing recently retired to an island off the Scottish coast searching for anonymity. However, the local police have been advised to look out for Stan Jones as a foot passenger or in a hire car on the ferry."

"You appear to have thought of most things, Freeman," said the Chief Constable. "But. I'm concerned we haven't started searching for this killer's vehicle. Have you issued an APB, Mercer?"

"We considered an alert broadcast to police officers within our area, sir, instructing the arrest of the suspect," said Geoff. "That approach has drawbacks. First, we don't know whether Jones is working in the UK, meaning we would need co-operation from various forces across the UK and mainland Europe. Second, because of his childhood experience, Stan Junior wasn't keen on having his photograph taken."

"He has a driving licence and a passport," said

Kenneth. "He must have provided legitimate photos for those."

"True," said Gus, "but what Geoff meant was Stan Jones has done everything possible to mask his scars. He wears gloves, whatever the weather. He has grown a beard. Although we can get a copy of the images he used for those official documents, we've got nothing current to distribute. So, do we stop every truck driven by a bearded man wearing a baseball cap and sunglasses in the hope the driver has significant scarring?"

"Registration number?" said Kenneth, opening his arms wide. "Surely, we know the registration of his tractor unit?"

"We know what it was when he bought it, sir," said Geoff. "However, he's avoided the nationwide CCTV coverage here in the UK, which might have tipped off detectives investigating the murders of those three girls."

"Which suggests he has a selection of vehicle registration plates, sir," said Gus. "The firms he works for wouldn't find it odd. Jones would automatically need to match the front and rear plates."

"He is clever," said Kenneth. "I'll give him that. I don't know how many firms he works for, but he needs to use the same false plates every time. That takes a good deal of planning and forethought."

"He will have several sets of foreign plates, too, sir," said Geoff. "It provides an extra layer of confusion for any traffic police watching for him."

"That's why we thought it best for you to hand everything over to Major Crimes," said Gus. "They have the necessary expertise to handle complex operations with multiple partners and international implications."

"What does that even mean?" asked Kenneth.

"No idea, sir," said Gus. "I only speak dinosaur. But that

sentence reminded me of what I hear from the bright young things who have reached the top of the tree in today's police service. In short, it's going to be a devil of a job. We're talking needle in a haystack territory, with thousands of vehicles that need pulling over to check whether the driver is our Stan Jones. But the alternative is just as risky. Neil Davis and Luke Sherman visited our suspect's father this morning. I haven't talked with them about everything they learned, but we know the Ponting Street address is young Stan's base of operations. He collects his mail on the rare visit he makes. One method he used to keep in touch with what was happening in Swindon was to pay for a subscription to the digital version of the Swindon Advertiser. That needs to be renewed in November. Gablecross can monitor the house and arrest Jones when he comes home."

Grab your copy...
vinci-books.com/intothesunlight